The Adventures of R'gal the Archangel

Book Three
Shamah and Anekah

by William Siems

The Adventures of R'gal the Archangel
Book Three Shamah and Anekah
Copyright © 2025 by William Siems
Published by William Siems

ISBN: 979-8-9900413-6-3

First printing - Spring 2025

Scripture quotations from the SUV (Siems Unauthorized Version) of the Bible

Contact the author at chayeem10@gmail.com

Cover and Interior design by Alane Pearce of Pearce Writing Services, LLC. apearcewriting@gmail.com

Cover art designed on Canva using AI

Dedication

In 2017, I published my first novel. It was forty-plus years in the making. This is number eleven, and without the faithful support of many this too would have remained just a dream or an hallucination. Thanks to the constant encouragement of my wife, the faithful few readers who kept asking, "What's next?" and my compassionately brutal editor, who somehow makes sense of my manuscript while maintaining a semblance of orthodoxy. A special thanks to my dog whom the neighbors use to take care of for me. She has gone to a "better place." Yes, I believe in animal heaven. Most of all, thanks to the One who continues to give me the inspiration of books to come, Jesus the Messiah.

Blessings…

Spring 2025
William Siems

Table of Contents

Preface

I have written a total of two apocryphal novels, three Biblical adventures, two archangel novels, and three contemporary Christian novels to date. This will be the third book that concerns the archangel who was slain in the rebellion. I know, that sounds like an oxymoron. I thought that they were supposed to be immortal too. Then, I'm just telling the story.

I'm not sure of your position on angels, let alone archangels, but my orthodoxy has been called into question before. So. I would suggest that you hold on…..because here we go.

Prologue

The portal opened and Rayeh walked through it. R'gal, the former archangel, sat at their favorite refreshment table. As R'gal got up to welcome Rayeh, another angel walked through the portal behind him. It was Shamah. He had been one of R'gal's favorite commanders before R'gal had been slain in the rebellion. R'gal embraced Rayeh while Shamah stood there with his mouth hanging open.

R'gal nodded his head once like a short bow, "Shamah, it is very good to see you."

Shamah nodded too and finally found his voice, "You were slain in the rebellion?" It was more of a question than a statement.

R'gal smiled, "That is true, but it is more difficult to kill an angel than it is just to slay him. I'm not even sure what that really means, even after having experienced it."

Shamah stepped forward to embrace him, "Why did you not come back to lead us?"

"He," and he inclined his head towards Rayeh, "had something else in mind for me to do."

Shamah whispered in his ear, "I'm so….so glad you're alive," then stepped out of the embrace.

Rayeh had filled their goblets, "Shall we take a seat?" They did. "R'gal has been on special assignment since being un-slain," and he smiled, "and I have brought you here, Shamah, to join R'gal and I in another special assignment." Shamah's eyes grew as wide as saucers.

He stammered, "Yes, my Lord. Of course, my Lord. Anything, anything at all. You have but to ask."

R'gal smiled slyly, "You may want to temper your excitement until you hear what it is." Shamah looked at R'gal sideways. He couldn't believe what he had just heard.

Rayeh addressed them both, "Are either of you omniscient?"

They both looked at each other, bewildered, "Of course not," Shamah voiced for both of them.

He continued, "You only know what you have seen, heard, been told, or experienced?" They both nodded, "So, it isn't surprising that you, Shamah, had not heard that R'gal had been un-slain," and he smiled at the word while they agreed. "So, let me recap some of the things you may or may not know. After man's disobedience and expulsion from the garden, things got worse, not better. Having given the enemy entrance into their world, he began with their first born and then many others after that to expand his evil plan. One of his primary plans became to mount a revolt on the heavens by creating a race in his own image. He would call them the 'Ashereem' when they matured. In order to finalize his union with the princes of the world he convinced some of them to allow his angels to unite with their daughters. The offspring would be half human, half divine."

Shamah looked at the ground, "We wondered why you didn't put a stop to such an abomination."

Rayeh explained, "We tried in a number of different ways, but to no avail. R'gal even got a chance to be a horse for awhile."

Shamah was appalled, "What, you're kidding?"

R'gal laughed, "No he isn't and he's just getting started."

Rayeh returned to his story, "Unknown to Lucifer, one of his two archangels, Haniel, fell in love with a princess, Judith. He married her and had a child by her. Unfortunately, she could have no other children after that child's birth. While technically Elah was one of the Ashereem, he never participated with them, but was raised separate from them by his father. The entrance of the Ashareem into manhood was celebrated by a contest. The winner would be awarded a special sword and a wife of Lucifer's choosing.

Also, unknown to Lucifer, Hathath had fathered a child of a lioness. Labee was the first of the Ariel, later to be worshipped by the Moabites. He too had grown to maturity, but was not considered an Ashareem or even known to them, seeing that he was the offspring of a lioness. Hathath also fathered two others.

Lucifer's other archangel, Raziel, had fathered Mekaroth. In the contest he defeated each of his opponents. When he had knocked out the last one and before he could be crowned the winner, Labee challenged Mekaroth in a 'fight to the death.' This fight would become the stuff of legend as Labee drove Makaroth all over the field with his stealth and prowess. Finally Labee knocked him to the ground, but before he could deliver the mortal blow, Elah stepped from the crowd with his father's singing sword in his hand, denied Labee his kill and engaged him in battle himself.

Lucifer offered Labee his own sword, as he proclaimed the battle would be to the death. Labee fought with Lucifer's own sword, but Elah finally slew him. As Labee crumpled to the ground, Hathath swore that Elah would pay. Rayeh seemed winded just the telling the story.

Shamah sat dumbfounded, finally caught his own breath to exclaim, "That really happened?"

R'gal squeaked, "Yes, I too was there, and it looked like things were headed for a happy ending as Elah fell in love with Judith's sister's daughter, Japhia. I was with Elah in the form of a dog,"

Shamah chortled.

R'gal said behind his hand, "You'll get your turn." He picked up the story again, "Elah was later killed by two Ariel, Labee's brothers and even though Haniel and I were able to kill them, Haniel never recovered from Elah's death."

Shamah and Rayeh both had tears in their eyes.

Shamah ventured, "And that brings us up to date?"

Rayeh smiled, "Almost. Haniel moved out of the house and later Japhia moved in to become the daughter Judith never had. R'gal joined them as another dog, a female of a different species from the last to keep Haniel from knowing of his return."

Shamah laughed as he shook his head, "A female dog. Will this never end?"

R'gal screwed up his face as he said, "I told you….."

Rayah went on, "He stayed with them until she met Enoch."

His eyebrows raised, Shamah asked, "THE Enoch?"

"Yes, that one! R'gal now lives with them and is due back there soon. We are almost done here. I want you to go back with him and meet Judith. You are to tell her that she will bear another child, a daughter."

Now Shamah was fully wide-eyed, "A daughter with Haniel? There has never been a female Ashereem."

Rayeh folded his hands on the table, "There will be another, Araphel, fathered by Lucifer himself. Haniel and Judith's daughter, Anekah, will be the balance. Both will be raised in secret until the time is ripe."

R'gal ventured, "I thought the Ashereem were an abomination?"

Rayeh sighed, "They were. That is why we tried to stop them. Now, we must work with the raw materials we have at our disposal." He sighed again, "Unless we want to start all over." He left it at that, "So, introduce Shamah to Judith and we'll see where things go from there."

A portal appeared behind them. They took a final pull from their goblets, stood, bowed towards Rayeh, and walked through the portal.

Part One
A New Assignment

Chapter One
Good News

They stepped through the portal and onto a forested lane that R'gal recognized. Shamah looked down and beside him walked a fawn colored Saluki, "R'gal, is that you?"

"Yes, and I hope your humility is intact. It is sure to be tested. This disguise will at least get us a hearing with Judith."

They turned into Judith's lane. It was still beautifully lined with a variety of colored rose bushes.

The guard looked at Shamah, who appeared as an athletic middle aged man, and then down at the dog. "Princess, is that you?" She approached, her tail wagging furiously. The guard knelt down, scratched and petted her. He looked at Shamah, "Are you with her?" and pointed towards the dog.

Shamah smiled for multiple reasons and nodded, "Yes, I am."

The guard stood, "Please wait here, and I will get my mistress." He returned moments later with Judith.

"Princess!" and she knelt down and hugged her. Then she looked at Shamah, "And you are with her?"

He held out his hand, "Shamah, my lady."

She held hers out too, he gently took her fingers, and brought them lightly to his lips. She added, "Welcome to my home, Shamah. Please follow me," and she led him to a sitting room, "Wine?"

Shamah nodded, "That would be wonderful." He pointed at Princess, "You know who that really is?"

Judith smiled coyly, "I do. Are you one of them too?"

Shamah returned the smile, "Yes, although not as important, I still represent Rayeh." He paused, "We bring good news. As you may have noticed and hoped, the way of a woman has been restored to you."

Tears filled her eyes, "Yes," she paused, "I was wondering how, and if it is even possible?"

His smile deepened, "The King of the Universe should not be able to restore your fertility?"

She looked down as a tear trickled down her cheek, "Well, when you put it that way."

Shamah went on, "I know that Haniel banished R'gal from his presence, but I was wondering if I could accompany you to him with this good news?"

She reached for a napkin and dabbed at her eyes, "I will send a herald telling him to expect us, but Princess cannot go with us."

Haniel met them at his door, looked sternly at Shamah as he spoke, "You are not just R'gal in a new disguise?"

"No, my Lord, I am not." He said reverently to Haniel, "I am Shamah and bring good news. You wife's fertility has been restored. You may father another child."

Stunned, it appeared Haniel was about to collapse.

"You're not serious!" He whispered as he looked at Judith.

She smiled shyly and looked away, "Yes, the way of a woman has been restored to me." He stepped forward and embraced her, still visibly shaken.

He met Shamah's gaze again, "Why would Rayeh do this for us?"

Shamah took a deep breath as if remembering the right words to say, "Some things must be earned, but favor may be given."

Haniel scowled, "And He would do this?"

Shamah smiled, "As your wife can testify, He already has."

Haniel turned and pulled Judith into his sitting room. He grabbed a decanter of wine and quickly poured some into three goblets. He handed one to his wife, one to Shamah, and took one himself and raised it, "To my son!"

Shamah countered, "It will be a daughter."

Both Haniel and Judith looked as if they had been slapped. "There are no female Ashereem," Haniel stammered.

Shamah took another deep breath, "Lucifer has fathered one himself. She will be a priestess of darkness. Your daughter will not. She will be wonderfully good, like your son."

The mention of Elah, his son, should have dampened the moment, but instead it made it even better. "Then, to my daughter."

Shamah whispered, "Anekah, her name will be Anekah."

Indignant, Haniel responded, "You're naming my daughter?"

Shamah spoke more confidently, "Hear me out, my Lord. Anekah is the joining of two words. Anek may be translated necklace and Kah is a brand, like you would use to brand cattle to identify them as your own. If Judith were to wear a necklace, the pendant would rest here," and Shamah pointed to his own lower neck. "Anekah will be born with a brand, a birthmark right here," and he pointed again, "marking her as Rayeh's from birth. If that is not true, feel free to name her whatever you like; but if it is true, please name her Anekah, so that she will know that she belongs to Him. She will not be a physical giant as the Ashereem grew to be, but a spiritual giant, and for good."

Both Haniel and Judith stood there, silent, fearfully breathless.

Finally Haniel spoke, "If it is as you have said, her name will be Anekah. I have a question. Have you spoken to R'gal concerning his service to us?"

Shamah waited a moment to consider his words, "Yes and I know he disappointed you," and he looked at the table.

Haniel looked deep into his eyes when Shamah raised his gaze. "Just as Rayeh is giving us a second chance, I would like to give heaven a second chance and ask you to be my daughter's godfather."

It was Shamah's turn to be stunned. He hadn't really considered this possibility, although he could feel Rayeh's smile as though he hid in the shadows. When he found his words, he replied, "I would be honored." He gulped. "I suppose you want me in the form of a dog."

They both smiled mischievously and nodded, "*Yes.*"

He replied resignedly, "I'll have to get back to you on that."

A portal opened behind him, he turned, and walked through it.

He stood at the refreshment table. Both R'gal and Rayeh sat there smiling. R'gal had that "*I told you so,*" look on his face.

Rayeh simply said, "R'gal will teach you all the dogginess you need to know." He got up and walked through a portal that had opened next to him.

Chapter Two
A New Dog
and New Princess

The Afghan Hound existed before there was an Afghan. Shamah stood before R'gal in all his long-haired glory.

R'gal laughed at him, "You look positively majestic."

Shamah snapped at him. "I should probably practice biting people," but R'gal had dodged the bite.

R'gal kept grinning, "That would not make a very good impression, especially when children are involved."

Shamah countered, "But it might as the protector of a child."

"Ah," R'gal sighed, "I'll give you that point. What should we call you?

Shamah thought a moment. "Since we named his daughter, Anekah for him, perhaps we ought to let him name me."

R'gal sighed again, "Splendid, but you should go now as she will be born tonight."

Shamah looked up at him, "Will they both be okay?"

R'gal looked off into the distance, "Yes, I believe that they will."

A portal opened behind Shamah, he turned, and trotted through it to end up in the familiar lane. He trotted between the rose bushes on the way up to the entrance to suddenly encounter the guard. He had forgotten about the guard.

"Now, what should I do?" he thought. The guard drew his sword. Shamah sat and then peaceably lay down like he didn't have a care in the world.

To his surprise the guard asked him, "Are you the dog I've been told to expect?"

He lifted his head and wagged his tail. He had forgotten they had talked about this months ago when he had been there in human form. The guard said sternly, "Wait here," and gestured with his hand for him to stay.

He returned with Haniel, "Are you the one?" Shamah again raised his head and wagged his tail. "Come then, follow me." Haniel turned and walked to the sitting room. Shamah followed him. "She is in labor, they told me it shouldn't be long." He paced the floor.

Shamah spoke to him, "Both Judith and Anakeh will be fine. I have it on the highest authority."

"Do you have a name or do I call you Shamah?" His words were short, but less fearful.

"Since your daughter's name was suggested, I thought you might like to choose mine." and Shamah sat.

"Stupid dog might be appropriate, but she would never call you that." He looked out the window. The sun had recently set. "How about 'twilight', Neseph?"

There seemed a grin in his voice, "Thank you for not naming me 'stupid dog'.

The cry of a child split the air. They both turned towards it. One of Judith's maids came into the room, "You have a healthy daughter, my Lord. Give us just a moment and then you may come and see her." She looked at the dog.

Shamah sat up as Haniel said, "His name is Neseph and he will be staying with us. Neseph, this is Abigail, one of Judith's maids."

Abigail knelt with her hand extended. Neseph sniffed it, then walked between it and her leg and leaned into her. She scratched and petted him, "Welcome, Neseph." He seemed to soak it all up.

One of the other maids entered the room, "You may come and see your daughter." She too looked at the dog.

Abigail helped her, "His name is Neseph and he will be staying with us." This maid too knelt, but Neseph followed on the heels of Haniel to go meet his daughter.

Judith sat propped up in bed with Anakeh at her breast. They both looked wonderful. No one would have imagined the ordeal that they had both just been through. Haniel leaned over and kissed his wife on the forehead, then gently stroked Anekah's surprisingly full head of hair.

Neseph was large enough that his head was above the edge of her bed and Judith commented, "Who's your friend?"

Haniel shook his head to clear the euphoria. "I'm sorry, this is Neseph, Anakeh's dog. He, too, just arrived."

He lay his head on the bed where she could reach him with her free hand.

As she scratched him behind the ear, and smiled "Welcome Neseph, we're so glad you have joined us."

Suddenly Abigail was at the door, "My Lord, Raziel is at the front door. Lucifer demands that you come to his court."

Haniel met Raziel at the door, "Do I need to bring protection?"

Raziel met his gaze, but weakly, "I didn't bring any to meet you."

Haniel scowled. "We will need to stop by my house and get my sword."

Raziel brought it out from behind his back and handed it to him. "While your soldiers are loyal to you, they allowed me to bring your sword to you for your own protection."

Haniel took the sword, buckled it on, and gestured out the door, "After you."

Two horses stood there, Raziel's and Haniel's, both held by a groom. They mounted and walked down the lane through the rose bushes. On the porch, behind them sat Neseph.

Raziel looked back over his shoulder, "New dog?"

Haniel smiled, "Yes."

Chapter Three
Lucifer's Court

They left their horses with a groom in Lucifer's courtyard and entered his palace. Everything in it was opulent, ostentatious, made to impress and demean the visitor. It had none of these effects on Haniel. He had been here before and nothing much had changed, other than a gold statue of Lucifer himself, holding a sword pommel in his right hand and the flat blade across his left, stood prominently in the middle of the foyer. You had to walk around it. Haniel was tempted to tip it over, but restrained himself. It was meant to intimidate, but again failed on Haniel. At the entrance to Lucifer's court chamber stood one of the Ashereem, a giant of a man, "No weapons are allowed in Lucifer's presence!" he commanded in a rough gravel-filled voice.

Raziel reached to unbuckle his sword,

Haniel just spoke forcefully, "Perhaps you'd like to try and take it from me?"

The Ashereem looked at Haniel, then to Raziel who was frantically shaking his head *"No, do not try!"* in little quick jerks. Raziel handed the Ashereem his sword. Haniel just brushed past him.

Lucifer sat on his ivory throne, but stood as they entered and spoke with fury, "You would wear a weapon in my presence?"

Haniel strode right up to the throne's dias, "Says the one who lent his sword against my son!" There was a bite to his words.

Lucifer took a slow deep breath and sat back down, "I am truly sorry for your loss. Even I do not command the Ariel." he said resignedly.

Haniel sneered, "I thought your intent was to rule everything!"

Lucifer sighed again, "An intent as yet unrealized. You could help me with that. I hear you have produced a female Ashereem."

Haniel smiled slightly, "Kudos to your network, but she is not an Ashereem, as my son was not an Ashareem. Besides," and he paused, "I have heard that you have produced your own female Ashereem."

The court was empty, but Lucifer's words as he looked to both Haniel and Raziel were menacing, "That information stays in this room. Besides, how could you know that?"

Haniel's smile deepened, "Yours is not the only network."

Lucifer tried to save face. "Perhaps we could train our daughters together?"

Haniel's smile darkened, "Most… certainly… not!"

Lucifer scowled, "Is it your intent to insult me?"

Haniel nearly laughed out loud, "No, only to be very clear."

"So, you intend to raise her at home?"

Haniel continued in his directness, "I do!"

"Who will instruct her?"

Haniel looked over Lucifer's head. "When it is time, I will find her a suitable tutor."

Lucifer spoke smugly, "I have the best!"

Haniel actually did chuckle, "I would expect you to think so."

Lucifer spoke curtly, "Sometimes you try my patience."

Haniel's smile never faltered, "As I said, just trying to be clear."

Lucifer hissed, "You are dismissed!"

Haniel bowed slightly and backed up towards the door until he was a few paces away.

Lucifer hissed again, "Raziel, you remain."

Haniel turned and left the court, smiling. Raziel nearly quaked in his boots.

"How could he know I have a daughter?" Lucifer demanded of Raziel.

He squeaked out, "I have no idea. I didn't know myself."

"See that you keep it quiet. It is critical to my next step in the conquest of all that there is."

Raziel pondered, "*All that there is? Could you be the Lord of what is not?*"

"Raziel," Lucifer broke his reverie, "Can you have him discretely followed?"

"Haniel? You must be joking?"

Lucifer spat, "I rarely joke!"

Raziel gulped, "Yes, my Lord."

"I expect your best, always!"

"Absolutely, my Lord."

Lucifer spat the words out, "You're dismissed,"

Raziel didn't need to hear that twice. He bowed deeply and retreated backwards, then turned and breathed a sigh of relief as he left the court.

Chapter Four
A Fresh Breeze

It didn't matter whether she was awake or asleep, Anekah was always reaching for Neseph. When she could speak, which was early for a normal child, she called him Seph. It was just easier. They were virtually inseparable. They often even bathed together, and of course ate, slept, and played together. His long hair was perfect for braids and bows. Fortunately that phase didn't last too long. It was evident that she considered Seph human. She talked to him as though he were human and listened to him as well, or at least seemed to do so too.

It was nice for her to have him as a companion, but Haniel and Judith both knew who he really was. They knew that she was fully safe, always. Anekah loved the outdoors and the two of them often wandered the nearby forests on Haniel's land. It was there that she learned that she could speak to others beside Seph. Anekah had just celebrated her third birthday, so this day the entire family tromped through the forest with her. She was running happily about twenty cubits in front of her parents, when she turned a corner and faced a lion. They heard her say, "Hello." They quickened their pace to catch up with her. Seph turned the corner first. He was surprised that he hadn't been warned, as she stood within easy striking distance of the lion.

It was then that he heard the lion speak, "Good morning, young one. Should you be out here by yourself?" That was when Seph had turned the corner, "Ah, I see that you are not."

Haniel and Judith now came around the corner at a run. Haniel's hand went to the hilt of his sword as the lion continued speaking to Seph and that angel part of Haniel, "That will not be necessary. If I had wished her harm, it would either be too late, or Rayeh would have warned you."

Anekah had her hand outstretched, "May I pet you?"

Seph stepped behind Anekah and between the lion and Haniel. He would have been in the way if Haniel had drawn his sword, but they both now perceived no threat.

Instead, Haniel reached back, wrapped his arm around Judith and said, "It will be okay."

She was visibly shaking.

The lion looked Anekah directly in the eyes, "Yes, you may pet me."

She advanced, let him smell her hand, and then stroked his nose. She moved her hand up the bridge between his eyes, stepped in, scratched his crown, then behind his ears, finally to hug him.

She turned to her parents, "I have a new friend." She paused, "I know how to speak to him."

Judith looked to Haniel, surprised.

Haniel remarked, "We did know that she'd be special."

Judith blinked, full of surprise, "She understands the language of the animals?"

He sighed, "So it would seem."

The lion cleared his throat. It rumbled, a bit like a growl, "I have come with news. Hathath sired another Ariel and has almost completed his training. Since you have killed all of his prior children, we fear that Luthur may be coming to attack your daughter. Therefore, I was sent to warn you. You need not be afraid, but you have been warned. We have heard about your daughter and are pledged to protect her as much as possible. That may only be by us providing you with information, but it will be better than nothing."

Feeling that they had enough adventure for one day they decided to return home, but before they left, Anekah gave the lion a final squeeze.

It felt so good to be in their own home, behind closed doors, although Anekah seemed unaffected by the entire adventure. As they lounged at the table, Haniel began by addressing Anekah, "Had you suspicioned that you could talk to animals?"

She scrunched up her face, "I have always spoken to Seph," as if that explained it.

Haniel looked sternly, "How did you know that the lion would not harm you?"

She met his gaze fully. "How did you? You did not draw your sword."

Haniel smiled, "True, I could sense it, on some level."

Anekah smiled, "Me too."

Haniel turned grave once again, "Perhaps we should limit your adventures in the forests."

She again met his gaze, "Father, that is not needed, I am protected."

Judith finally spoke, "What do you think that means, that you are protected?"

She turned her gaze on her mother and smiled. "Animals love me, Seph loves me, Rayeh loves me, they all watch out for me."

Judith sighed, "While that is true, we may still want to be more careful."

Anekah put her fists on her hips, "Careful is for a baby, I am no baby."

Judith smiled, "Yes, but you could be careful for your mother, couldn't you?"

She thought a moment, then her look softened, "Yes, for you, I can be careful."

Chapter Five
The Refreshment Table

Shamah walked through the portal to find Rayeh at their favorite table of refreshments. Shamah jumped right in, "You knew about Hathath and the Ariel that is seeking to find Anekah?"

Rayeh furrowed his brows, "Of course."

Shamah furrowed his own, "And you didn't think I needed to know that information?" Then he remembered who he was talking to. "I'm sorry.... I spoke rashly."

Rayeh sighed, "It's okay, remember, I know you are only an angel."

Shamah shook his head, "And you are only the King of the entire universe."

Rayeh smiled, "Yes!"

Shamah, again with furrowed brows, an thought out loud, "Do we need to assign more angels to protect her?"

Rayeh pretended to think for a moment, then chuckled, "No, with all of the animals that are falling in love with her, and you, and her father, that should prove sufficient. By the way, how is life as a dog?"

Shamah looked at the table, "Humbling."

Rayeh smiled again, "Anything else."

He looked up and to the right, "Besides Anekah, it seems I am generally ignored. I think that they forget that I am there. It is a good disguise for gaining intelligence." He brightened up.

Rayeh cocked his head slightly to the left, "And being scratched behind the ear?"

Shamah, sighed, "Yes, I have never known love like that before. It's…." and he paused, "hard to put into words."

"It's touching," Rayeh laughed at his own pun.

"So, what's next?" Shamah inquired sheepishly.

"Wouldn't you like to know!"

Shamah nodded furiously.

"You have never met an Ariel, have you?"

"No, I haven't. What should I expect?" He was most curious.

"You should expect the unexpected. Graft together a lion and an angel and what do you get? You get the unexpected. But you can talk to Haniel, he has faced them before."

Shamah's curiosity still burned, "Why should Hathath try again? He has already lost three of his children to Haniel and his son."

"Yes, but Hathath has lived alone with the animals a long time. He has become more like them than the angel he used to be. Now he is brutal, cunning, territorial, and worse." Rayeh confided. "And if that is not enough, add Anekah into the mix… more unexpected."

There was a long pause, then Shamah asked, "Where does my sword go when I change into the form of a dog?"

Rayeh smiled, "Does it really matter?"

Shamah looked at the ground, "If I need to attack quickly. I just wondered."

Rayeh looked down at the sword strapped to Shamah's thigh,."It will always be there when you change into your human form. That's enough, isn't it?"

Shamah took a long slow breath, "I guess so."

"Well, It's about time that you were back, although it will only seem like you were outside long enough to do your doggie duty."

Shamah realized that Rayeh smiled a lot. He thought, *"I suppose that is a good thing."* A portal opened, he took a final pull from his goblet, stood, and walked through it to emerge as a dog on the other side. He walked between the roses up to Haniel's front door, where the guard stooped down to pet him. There were some good things about being a dog. Most people genuinely adored you and showed it. He went to find Anekah.

Chapter Six
Luthur

The life of an Ariel was a lonely one. Both animals and angels considered you an abomination, whereas the regular Ashereem were esteemed as giants, beings of heroic exploits. As an Ariel, you were not! For now, Luthur was seen as a monster. He was however, an incredibly accomplished swordsman. So, he hoped he would fare better than his brothers against the archangels. He couldn't know for sure, as there were no archangels with whom to spar. His oldest brother had nearly killed the son of a fallen one, and his two older brothers had killed the son of the other fallen one, before they were later dispatched themselves.

The best Luthur could do was to spar against his father, who was at least an angel, although that was a far cry from fighting a real archangel. As an Ariel, he seemed to have inherited the best of both worlds. Lion from the shoulders up, he had the senses and savagery of the lion. The rest of him took the form of an angel or a giant of a man. He had heard the stories of his brothers battles. There was Labee's victory over Raziel's son that was cut short by Elah, the son of Haniel. Then there was the attack of Labah and Laesh on Elah and his sweetheart, Japhia, at Haniel's training ground. His brothers were now dead and Japhia had moved in with Judith.

Having heard that Haniel had now sired a daughter, Luthur believed that an attempt on her life would produce a more satisfying result than simple revenge for his brothers deaths.

Luthur was a master of stealth. He had honed his skill to move soundlessly through any terrain until it seemed almost magical. What he was unprepared for was the animal network that surrounded Haniel's daughter, Anekah. He often traveled through the forests that bordered around Haniel's land, especially near his training ground, with seeming impunity, until the day he was approached, nearly as soundlessly as he traveled, by a large adult lion. Luthur turned to his left to find him standing motionless, just out of striking distance.

Luthur spoke menacingly, "Do you have any idea who I am?"

Ladub spoke casually, "Of course I do. You are Luthur, the abomination sired upon a lioness by Hathath."

Luthur bristled to his full height, "Some call me a god, and you would dare to speak to me in that tone?"

Ladub just sat there, glee resonating in his voice, "You are no god and never will be. You obviously do not know the God of the Universe or you would not so carelessly compare yourself to Him." Luthur drew his sword, but Ladub continued, "That would be a very bad idea. Anekah lives under our protection. To threaten her would incur the wrath of every animal in this forest. You would stand no chance of defeating us all, let alone of reaching her."

Luthur slowly sheathed his sword and spoke angrily, "You may leave now!"

Ladub turned and padded away.

Luthur thought to himself, *"Now what?"*

Then he too silently left the forest and went to where he had set up his base of operation. It was a cave in the side of a hill that was obscured from normal view. You had to know it was there. He stepped inside and waited until his eyes adjusted. In the dim light from the entrance he could now navigate to his fire pit. He built and lit a fire, then sat on a bench he had made with his own hands. His father had taught him how long ago. He sat and contemplated his next move. He needed to wait until the animal observers had relaxed their guard. He was well adapted to waiting. He had prepared and waited all these years. There was no way he would lesson his chances of success by being in a hurry. While he waited, he decided to travel to the East and see what other skills he could develop.

Chapter Seven
Return to the Practice Field

For her twelfth birthday Anekah's father gave her a bow. The arrows he would teach her to manufacture herself. They secured the wood for the shafts. Some of her bird friends provided the feathers for the fletching. Then, at her father's command, their smithy taught her how to make arrow-heads and nocks. It began with the molds, delicately hammered out of rock: *chip, chip, chip.* At least she was not required to mine the ore. She was, however, required to oversee the fires that melted it, then to pour it into the mold. It needed to cure overnight, but that afternoon they trimmed the feathers and mounted them as the fletching for the arrows. She was preparing her first dozen. They would not be the broad-headed arrows capable of slaying a large animal, but the smaller heads used in target practice, which could still drop a smaller animal.

She had carved the arrows and crafted the heads so that they actually screwed onto the shafts. They were applied with a type of resin that made them nearly impossible to re-move. It bound the metal and the wood into one substance.

It was similar with the nocks although they did not need to screw on. Haniel had thought, at first, about giving her a dagger. He could not picture her as a swordsman, but a dagger would be fitting. Then the picture of her shooting a bow had interrupted his thinking. While she was too friendly with the animals to hunt them, the beauty and delicacy of archery had stayed with him. One day, on a lark, he had handed her his long bow. She took it like she was born to it and even while it was his heavy hunting bow, she had pulled the string to her cheek with seemingly little effort. It was then that he realized she had done it left-handed. He did not ever recall having met a left-handed archer. How fitting, it seemed, that his daughter should be the first and perhaps only one.

While Judith would not have been pleased for Haniel to have taught Anekah the sword, she was exceptionally pleased that he would be teaching her the bow. She even accompanied them to the practice field for her first lesson. He had crafted a shoulder quiver for her, an arm guard to protect her from the string, and a hand hold that laced around the bow to provide both a comfortable grip and a place between the wood and her hand for the arrow to rest before it took flight. Haniel had attached a leather target to three hay bales stacked about forty cubits away. An added bonus to her being left-handed to his right, she could mimic him with her bow as he'd demonstrated with his own. He put four arrows within the span of a hand down range and then they went and retrieved them. She was a wonderfully attentive pupil. Her first volley of four arrows matched his own, all within less than a hand's span. It was remarkable. They practiced for an hour, until the pattern of her arrows in the target began to expand a little with fatigue. He went with her the next day and the next, until she was allowed to go to practice on her own, accompanied only by Seph.

The lion, Ladub, visited them occasionally. The only news was that it seemed Luthur had left and not returned. There was no news of him at all. Perhaps that is what accounted for their slowly growing lapse in security.

Anekah entered the practice field with Seph at her side. Haniel had put a new target on the hay bales, as her last one was riddled with holes by her consistency. She had finished her first volley of four arrows and was about to retrieve them.

Seph sat up quickly and began to growl. Luthur stepped out of the forest to foolishly give up his advantage. If he had charged out of the forest to attack her, he could have quickly dispatched her. Perhaps he wanted to gloat.

He sneered, "Your brother killed mine. Your father killed one of my other brothers. Now, I will kill you."

She actually smiled at him, "If you will consider the target, I'm a pretty good shot."

His sneering continued, "Yes, but how fast are you?" It was then he realized that she had already nocked another arrow. He furrowed his lion brows.

"Faster than you think, but…" and she reached over and lay the bow and its arrow down as she said, "Seph, lie down."

Seph couldn't believe what he had just heard. He quickly raised a prayer to Rayeh and lay down.

Doubt crossed Luthur's face, "You would give up your seeming advantage?"

Her smile broadened, "It was more than just a seeming advantage, but I have a question for you."

Now it was astonishment that crossed his face, "What?" Then the sneer returned, "You have a question?"

She took a deep breath, "Yes. Have you ever been loved?"

He reacted as if he had been slapped, "What?"

She repeated herself, "Have you ever been loved?" She delivered the words with such compassion that he remained stunned. "All your life you have trained for this moment, but is this how you want to define your life?"

Suddenly his resolve seemed to be crumbling. He tried to stand taller, "My father bred me, trained me, all for this moment!" Yet it seemed somehow hollow.

"Yes, but did he love you?" The words continued to ring in the air. She motioned to Seph as she said, "Stay," and began walking towards the Ariel. He had drawn his sword when he emerged from the woods. As she got closer, it fell from his hand. She stood before him, "May I lay my hand on your forehead?" He nodded almost imperceptibly and lowered his head. When her hand touched his head he began to slightly shake and fall to his knees. "It's okay," she intoned, and then she began to sing,

"Forged in the darkness an anvil of pain
  Hammered in anger and hate.
A weapon of loss, grief, and revenge
  Forced by the dark one to wait.
All of this darkness seemed to converge
  with the aloneness of night.
Ugly, ungodly mortally wounded
  It slithered its way to the light.
Now it is seen, called forth by wonder
  Called by the heavens above
Once birthed in darkness, called forth by beauty
  How will you know…
  How can you ever…
  Regain your life in His love."

The echo of words, the music she had crafted, seemed to fill the void left by the end of the song. Luthur's great head lay in her arms, sobbing. Seph himself, lay there in awe wondering, *"What have I just witnessed?"* When the creature's sobs subsided, Anekah lifted his head and looked deep into his eyes, "Luthur, you have a destiny. You do not need to kill me, like your father told you. Some of the giants have gone out to perform exploits and to make names for themselves. You need to simply pick a people and become their hero. Fight for them, make a name for them, and in the process find your place in the annals of their legends. Win their love, prove worthy of their reverence, become the Ariel you were always meant to be."

Luthur struggled to his feet, picked up his sword and sheathed it. Then he reached out to take Anekah's head in his hands. He bent and touched his nose to her forehead as he said, "Thank you," turned and strode back into the forest.

Anekah walked to the target, like nothing had happened, removed her four arrows, put them in her quiver, returned to pick up her bow and said, "Now that was interesting." Then to Seph, "You can get up now. Oh, thank you for understanding."

Seph replied, "I didn't understand. I didn't have a clue. I just didn't get any other instructions but to obey you."

She laughed, "Well, thanks for that!"

Seph spoke reverently, "You do know who I really am?"

She looked at him, up and down, "Besides my friend, I need know nothing else."

Seph turned into his human form, complete with sheathed sword. "I am an angel, like your father."

She took a slow breath and spoke again, "Not to seem insulting, but are you also one of the fallen?"

Now he turned into his angelic self, nearly nine cubits tall with wings and all.

She stood looking up, then said, "I like you fine as just a dog."

Seph sighed and returned to his dog shape. She stepped to him, knelt, and hugged him, "Easier to hug as a dog too."

He just shook his head.

Anekah didn't say anything about the ordeal until after supper. As they lounged at the table she started, "Seph and I had an interesting afternoon at the practice field. Luthur showed up." Her father almost bolted upright, but she consoled, "It's okay father... I'm still here for starters." Then she went on to explain the encounter while Haniel kept looking at Seph with eyes that thought, *"Weren't you there to protect her?"*

Judith finally asked, "How did you know what to say?"

Anekah looked over to the corner of the table where they left a plate for any stranger, should he join them for supper, "It just seemed like what Rayeh would have said and done. Apparently it was, seeing the result that it had. He turned an enemy into a friend, imparting to him his identity and destiny. Doesn't that sound like something Rayeh would do?" They had to agree, it did. Then she added, "Afterwards, Seph revealed to me that he is an angel. I think that is meant to be comforting," and she laughed as though it really didn't matter one way or the other.

Chapter Eight
I'm Eighteen Now

The years had been very good, wonderful actually. Anekah grew in favor with man and beast, and turned into an amazing archer. She seemed to love archery almost as much as she loved Seph and her family. That is why they were all dumbfounded when she announced after supper, "Tomorrow is my eighteenth birthday and I am going on a journey."

Her parents responded almost in unison, "What?"

She smiled, she had such an engaging smile, "Yes, to celebrate my becoming a woman, I am going away."

Judith started to worry, "Where? For how long?"

Haniel was a little more rational and pragmatic, "And why are you doing this?"

She simply replied, "I am supposed to."

He countered, "Who says so?" She just pointed up. Haniel looked at Seph, "And you are just going to go along with this?"

Seph looked down to the ground, "Not my call."

Haniel looked skyward, "And I'm supposed to be okay with this?"

Seph interjected, "Careful, he is still the King of the Universe and he has just given you eighteen years beyond your wildest dreams."

Judith reached out to grasp Haniel's forearm, "There is that." She looked skyward herself, "And we are truly grateful."

A portal opened and Rayeh stepped through. Haniel fell to his knees and spoke to the ground, "Are you allowed to even be in the same room with me?"

Rayeh smiled like the sun emerging from behind a cloud, "Is there anywhere that I am not allowed?"

Haniel didn't know how to answer that, but still averted his eyes. Anekah ran up to Rayeh and embraced him.

He responded almost as if surprised, "Wow, it's been a long time since that has happened."

She put her head on his shoulder and he held it there while he spoke. "I have an assignment for your daughter. Well, maybe more than one. If you could spare her and entrust her to me."

Judith looked hopefully into Rayeh's eyes, "How long will she be gone for? When will I see her again?"

Rayeh looked away as if thinking, "I don't usually share the future," and he paused, "but Judith, you are mortal. You will not meet her again in this life. Haniel, on the other hand," and he left the sentence open-ended.

Anekah stepped out of her embrace with Rayeh and walked slowly to her mother and embraced her. "Mother, I have so much to be grateful for. While I am only half human, physically, you have made me much more than that in totality. I am ever indebted to you," and she paused before adding, "both."

Rayeh had watched the entire scene. "The other good news is Seph will be going with her." Rayeh turned and stepped through a portal.

Judith stepped over to take Haniel's hand, looked at Anekah, "So, this is goodbye?"

Anekah looked them both in their eyes. "No, this is the eaglet standing on the edge of the nest, ready to be launched into flight, and her eagle parents not frantically holding her back, but releasing her to join the sky."

They both took a deep breath and Haniel spoke for them, "Then," and he paused, "we release you."

Anekah chuckled, "Can I sleep here one more night and leave in the morning?"

They joined her chuckle, "Of course you can." She stepped into their embrace and they held each other for a long time.

She finally disentangled herself and turned to the dog, "Okay, Seph, one more night of luxury." She turned back to them, "Goodnight," clasped her hands together almost as if in prayer, turned away with a, "Come on Seph," she left them standing by the dinner table.

Judith turned to Haniel and began to weep softly. Haniel held her close, until the sobbing subsided, and then they too went to bed. When Haniel went to check on Anekah, early the next morning, she and Seph were gone.

Chapter Nine
A Moabite God

Luthur sat on a bench in the sun, outside, in the back of his palace, overlooking his garden, when he heard one of his soldiers coming up behind him. He had heard him approaching, so he wasn't surprised. Rather, he called out to the soldier before he was close enough to speak, "Mehujael, what is it?"

Mehujael, quaking in his boots, replied, "I am sorry to interrupt you, my Lord. There is a woman here, with her dog. They are seeking audience."

That was as far as he got. Luthur pivoted on the bench soundlessly to face the soldier as he called out, "Anekah? Send her in and have chilled wine brought to us."

His head was still bowed, "Yes, my Lord."

Mehujael returned escorting Anekah, the dog, and a servant carrying a tray of wine and goblets. Because he was so tall, Luthur remained seated, but stretched our his hands to welcome her. "Ah, Anekah, as you can see, your words were prophetic." She knelt before him, but he reached forward, lightly grasped her shoulders, "You need never to kneel before me."

She looked him directly in the eyes, while the soldier and servant's heads remained bowed, "It was an expression of respect."

He grumbled a low growl, "Which I receive, thank you." He motioned for her to sit beside him. "Seph," and he motioned to her feet.

Seph lay down at her feet and looked up to him, "I am honored that you remember my name."

Luthur replied, "I remember everything about that day. My life was entirely changed from that day onward. The Moabites now worship me, but not just because no man can match me in combat. They worship me for the kind of being I have become thanks mostly to you," and he looked to Anekah, "and that day." Then he remembered the soldier and the servant, "You may place the tray next to Anekah and then you may leave us." The servant did so and the two of them backed out of Luthur's presence. "So, what brings you, and he," he said humorously, "to the palace of a god?"

Anekah had poured the wine and handed him a goblet. He had the hands and forearms of an angel, being a lion only down to his elbows. "We are on a mission from the God of the Universe."

He looked up, "Oh, from Him." He was not speaking sarcastically, but almost reverently, "and what is the mission?"

She looked up too, "You know of Methuselah?"

He nodded.

"I am to find one of his sons, Lahab."

"He lives north of Mount Nebo near Rabbah. Would you like me to have you taken there? Godliness has its privileges."

She reached over and placed her hand on his, "No, I have to find it by myself, but thanks for the information. Have you found love?"

He looked at her hand, then caught her eyes, the ones that looked into your soul. "Worship, fear, but not love yet. You could stay here and rule as my queen."

There were tears in her eyes as she broke his gaze, "As wonderful as that would be," she looked up, "sadly, no. There seems to be some urgency to this meeting and an escort would not be appropriate. I do have the animals, remember."

"Ladub?" he asked.

"No, his son though, and Seph. Did you know that Seph was an angel?" she added.

"Still am," he snuck in.

His chuckle sounded like a growl, "An appropriate disguise."

"Heh…" Seph feigned offense.

"No offense intended, just an observation." Luthur returned.

Anekah wiped her eyes and her smile returned, "I have an idea. The only angel you ever sparred with was you father, right?" Luthur nodded. "How would you like to spar with an un-fallen angel?"

He looked to Seph, "As a dog?"

She laughed, "No, silly, as an angel?" She looked at Seph.

"You're kidding?"

She shook her head.

Seph looked up with a quick prayer and a sigh of resignation, "He said it's okay."

Luthur called out to his soldier, "Mehujael!"

He stepped through the doorway, "Yes, my Lord."

Luthur stood, "We are going down through the garden to my training area. I do not want to be disturbed."

Mehujael responded, "Of course, my Lord."

Luthur took a final swallow from his goblet and set it on the bench. Anekah stood and did the same. Seph just got up. They took the winding staircase down to the garden.

Chapter Ten
Another Training Ground

Luthur led them along a wide graveled path between rows of countless flowers; tulips, roses, chrysanthemums, carnations, and more. It reminded Anekah powerfully of home, inhaling the fragrance deeply with every breath. The path entered a forest for about a stadia and then emerged into an area of well-packed earth, two hundred cubits square. Luthur turned around towards them, "Do you need to warm up?"

Anekah took a step back, leaving Seph between her and Luthur, who drew his sword and took his stance. Suddenly, between them stood an angel, nearly nine cubits tall, with wings and all, dressed in battle armor. Before he drew his sword, he offered his hand, "Shamah."

Luthur sheathed his sword and grasped Shamah's forearm. "You are a little taller than I expected."

He smiled, "I am pure angel, you are half lion. Do I need my battle armor?"

"Will it slow you down?" asked Luthur hopefully.

His smile broadened, "Not so as you would notice."

"Then it is entirely up to you." Luthur's confidence seemed to be growing.

"You'll have to excuse me, I may be a little rusty. I don't get much of a chance to spar as a dog," and Shamah chuckled.

"I'm sure it will all come back to you." Luthur hoped it would take a while.

"Sure, probably like riding a horse." Shamar sighed contentedly as he drew his sword.

It was not one of the singing swords that the archangels possessed, yet it was nearly as fine a blade. Luthur possessed a blade crafted by the hidden forest smith Robsar, like his brothers had all possessed. It was nearly as fine a blade as the angel's and also, because Shamah did not use a singing sword, it did not sing. He drew it and the two of them took their stances. They reached out and touched blade to blade in respect, then stepped back.

Luthur could have attacked ferociously and tried to beat Shamah into submission, but he wanted to get the feel of him first. His attack was more calculated and slower than Shamah had expected. Six blows at an even cadence, but at different angles. Shamah easily parried them all and then disengaged. Now it was his turn and he delivered his six blows. Luthur countered each of them, but it was more difficult than he expected. The power hidden in each blow surprised him.

Enough with the small stuff, Luthur attacked with fierce directness: blow, after blow, after blow, after blow. Shamah gave ground to him initially, until they reached about the middle of the training ground and then executed a move that defied logic as much as it defied gravity. At least he wasn't using his wings. Luthur was not winded, but he was frowning. Shamah had obviously remembered his rarely practiced swordplay. He executed another gravity defying twist as he countered. *"How could he do that and maintain his balance?"* Luthur was getting frustrated, but he knew better than to fight with his anger. This time when Shamah executed his gravity defying pivot Luthur thought he had anticipated it, only to find himself disarmed. He stood there trying to comprehend what had just happened.

Shamah smiled. He wasn't even winded. "Lucifer taught me that one. Of course it was before he was fallen. I'm not sure he could still do it himself."

Luthur spoke with admiration, "Could you teach it to me?"

"And lose my advantage?" His smile broadened. "I'd be happy to teach it to you. It is actually simpler than it looks. In fact, that is its secret." For the next hour, Luthur concentrated on learning this new twist and parry from Shamah.

Meanwhile, over in the corner, Anekah sat on the ground with a lion beside her and his cub in her lap. When the two were finally through sparring, they walked over to her.

Shamah spoke first, "Ladub, is that you?"

The lion replied, "No sir, I am his son and this is my son." He laid a paw on the cub that was nearly purring in Anekah's lap.

Luthur spoke curtly, "What are you doing on my training ground?"

The lion stood, "We heard that Anekah was here and wanted to meet her."

Luthur looked at Shamah, who shrugged his shoulders.

Anekah spoke softly, "And they brought news from home." Shamah returned to his dog form and the lion seemed startled. Anekah noticed and scratched him behind the ear. "It's okay, I find his angel form more startling."

The lion stood, "I am Kilyah, son of Ladub, and this is my son, Benoni. We have been asked to accompany you partway on your journey."

Luthur spoke, "They are headed north past Mount Nebo to a place near Rabbah, where Methuselah lives."

Kilyah's ears perked up at that. "Methuselah, the long living one, we know of him. I can send on ahead for the animals to give us his exact location."

Luthur pointed, "There is a game trail that will take you to a path that will lead you in the right direction. I am assuming you want to stay off the main roads?"

Shamah finally spoke, "Yes, we do, and thanks for the lesson."

Luthur looked at Anekah, "Can you stay and have supper with me? I can also send some provisions with you."

Anekah looked up and then back into Luthur's eyes, "Thank you for the kind offer, but I will actually be fasting during the journey."

"It will be a journey of over one hundred and sixty stadia. At a pace on trails through the forest it will take you up to three days," Luthur commented with concern.

A smile again graced her face, "Yes, I appreciate that, but I have been assured that all will be well."

"Can I at least offer you a bed for this evening and you can leave in the morning?" He was still concerned.

She had been looking over his head again and sighed, "Yes, that would be most kind of you." She looked at Kilyah and his son, "Can we meet here in the morning, just after sunup?"

Without hesitation, he said, "Yes, we will be here."

She gestured towards where they had entered the training ground, "Then, Luthur, show us to our beds, please."

Luthur looked to Kilyah and Benoni, "Take good care of this one, there is no one else like her."

They both bowed as Kilyah replied, "Yes, we know, and yes, we will."

Chapter Eleven
A Northward Journey

Luthur, Anekah, and Seph met Kilyah and Benoni at the training ground. She hugged Luthur closely, burying her face in his mane and then let him go.

Facing him she said, "I do not know if we will meet again, but it has been a great pleasure to know you."

He gave a low whimper, "The pleasure was mine." Then he turned to Seph, "and thanks for the lesson in swordsmanship."

Seph yipped, "That was my pleasure. I hope we do meet again. I have a few more sword secrets up my sleeve," and he rubbed his forelegs together.

Luthur turned towards Kilyah with, "Then, I release them into your care."

Kilyah responded, "Thank you," and he turned towards the others. "Shall we be off?

Together they turned towards the path. Kilyah nearly commanded, "Benoni, take point. I will take the rear guard." Seph stepped up beside Benoni.

"And I get to walk alone? I don't think so," and Anekah held back to walk beside Kilyah. They set off at a moderate pace and soon the cubits turned into stadia. The game trail merged into the path through the forest and it was now easier to walk side by side.

Anekah chuckled, "Shall we sing a song?"

Steph joined her chuckle, "I hope no one can hear us."

Step by step we cover ground
  terrain we do not recognize.
The trees and bushes all around
  that cover and obscure the skies.

Chorus
It's just a walk, we're on a walk,
  a walk and nothing more.
We're slowly moving on ahead,
  unknowing where the angels soar
The song that's swirling in our heads
  is spilling out of heaven's door.
So keep on walking, walking, walking,
  until we reach the other shore.

The day is hot, the night is cold
  our feet are tired and sore.
No time to stop and see the sights
  or learn our neighbors lore.

So keep on walking, walking, walking
  until we reach that distant shore.

Anekah sang in her sweet soprano voice, while Seph howled in something that approached harmony. The lions grunted in time and on beat to provide some percussion.

The animals actually covered up the song in such a way that if you were a stadia away it didn't sound like a song at all. They continued most of the morning until they found a clearing with a small spring and the lions went in search of their lunch. They would have brought some back for Anekah, but she was fasting, and as an angel, Seph did not require food. After a brief respite in the meadow, they were off again northward. This time, instead of a song, Anekah produce a small wooden flute to softly accompany their walking.

"Ah," Seph muttered, "I wondered when you would honor us with your flute."

She stopped a moment. "It was that or let you compose a song of romping through the brush chasing small animals."

Seph *"Hrumphed"* as she began her music once again.

Its lilting melody melted the stadia away, until Benoni returned with the news. "There is a meadow a short way off the path up ahead that should provide a perfect spot for this evening's camp." He led them to it and Anekah made a small fire while the lions again left to find their supper.

They also brought back a young man they all recognized. "Look who we found sitting on a log just up around the next bend."

Anekah scrambled to her knees and Seph put his head between his paws where he lay in what resembled a posture of supplication. "My Lord?" Anekah intoned.

"Please," Rayeh said, "thank you for showing me these gestures of respect." He chuckled and waited while they got comfortable once again. "I had hoped you would find this spot, but didn't want my presence here to make you think someone had already taken it, so I waited up ahead for the lions to find me. As Anekah has shared with you, you are seeking Methuselah, but it is his son, Lahab, who will find you late tomorrow on this same pathway. After tomorrow's lunch, the lions will take to following you two in the woods." He looked at Anekah and Seph, "Do you trust me?"

They were both shocked, and said almost in unison, "Of course we trust you."

Rayeh sighed, "This may prove difficult. Tomorrow will be cloudy, overcast, with the threat of rain. You will come to a spot where the path takes a sharp turn to the East, punctuated by a white birch tree. At that point, there will be a crack of lightening, the sound of thunder, and a branch of the birch tree will fall and hit you in the head. Anekah, you will lay on the path unconscious and, Seph, you will stand guard over her nearly lifeless form. You won't have to wait too long for Lahab to appear. What happens next? I have it on good authority that you can make things up as you go. You won't have too much difficulty as you will be suffering from partial amnesia from the blow to your head. Any questions?" They just cringed.

Kilyah asked, "May we follow them to where she is taken?"

"From a discrete distance and silently in the woods, yes, but remember that you are lions and will be treated as such by any other human besides us. Have a good rest. Tomorrow is a big day." A portal opened behind him, "Perhaps a hug is in order before I go?" Rayeh hugged Anekah, reached down to scratch Seph behind the ear, he turned, and stepped through the portal.

Chapter Twelve
Lahab

A nekah did sleep rather well, out there in the country air. She had the soft grass, a warm blanket, a bundled coat for a pillow. You would have thought she was home. The next day dawned as Rayeh had said, overcast with a threat of rain. It was after lunch, no food, just a rest stop and a crystal clear spring, that she saw the white birch tree up ahead. She slowed, there was the flash of lightening, crack of thunder, and a branch of the tree struck Anekah, knocking her to her back on the ground. She awoke to Seph's low growl, but didn't open her eyes. All she heard, in addition to that, was a calm soothing voice.

Lahab told his soldiers to go back around the corner and leave him to face the dog and the fallen woman alone. "Easy boy, it's okay. I won't hurt your mistress."

He cleared away the tree branch, slowly knelt on the path, one hand on the dirt, the other hand out before him, palm extended. He waited. The dog warily crept forward to smell his palm, finally licked it and sat just in front of the fallen woman. She was breathing shallowly. Lahab could see the small, but slow rise and fall of her chest. He crawled to her, lifted her head, then, grasping her under the arms pulled her to his chest.

He whispered, "It will be all right. I am here. You are safe. You are rescued." Then Lahab called softly back over his shoulder, "Mattan, send two man back and bring me a stretcher. Hurry!" He heard the scurry of feet retreating as he reached out to the dog and motioned him to come closer. Seph approached them and nuzzled her in his arms.

Lahab called again softly, "Mattan, bring Bedad and slowly walk by us to protect us from the south. Leave the others to protect us from the north."

The dog lifted his head and was on high alert as the two men slowly, cautiously walked around the three of them to station themselves just to the south. He heard the scurry of feet approach and stop just around the corner.

One of the soldiers called, "We have the stretcher, my lord."

Lahab cautioned, "Bring it slowly along the path to the west of us." He addressed the dog, "I am going to lift your mistress." The dog stepped back to give him room. He had her at waist height when the stretcher arrived along side of them. He slowly laid her on the stretcher, then moved to take the southern end of the pole handles by her head.

He addressed the soldier at the other end of the stretcher, "Begin walking slowly back to the palace, trying not to bounce or sway the stretcher too much. Mattan, run back and have my wife and one of her handmaids prepare a room for our guests." He turned his head to the dog, "Come." and the dog walked along side of the stretcher. Anekah continued to lay still and breathe shallowly. Their slow march seemed effective and they were soon at the palace.

Ashima, Lahab's wife, met them at the entrance to the palace. It was not magnificent nor ostentatious, but possessed a simple beauty contained in the harmony and balance that it tried to display. It would be easy for a traveller to feel at home in this place. "Take her to the room with the eastern exposure. It receives the most natural light."

They laid her gently on the bed and the men left her to the ministrations of Ashima and her handmaid. They washed the dirt off her face and she continued to play the unconscious young woman. Finally they left her alone with the dog, who could not be coaxed from her bed. Once they were gone Anekah confirmed with Seph, "Are they gone?"

"Yes, mistress, they have left us alone," Seph whispered.

"How long was I out?" she asked him.

Concern laced his voice, "Not long."

"Things are a little foggy." She confessed.

"Will you be all right?" He queried.

"I think so." She drifted off for a few moments.

When they next checked, she was awake, fondling the dog's head as it lay on the bed.

Chapter Thirteen
Lahab and Ashima's Home

Anekah still appeared somewhat bewildered when the handmaiden slowly opened the door. Seeing that the girl was awake, she went to fetch her mistress.

Ashima, herself, entered slowly. "You are safe, my child. This is my home. You were found unconscious in the wilderness, apparently from a blow to the head. Can I get you something to eat or drink?"

Anekah looked around the room as though she couldn't quite see or make sense of her surroundings. "Some bread and wine if I may? I can't remember when I last ate."

Ashima turned and spoke to her handmaid, "Bella, please fetch us some bread and wine." She then turned to Anekah, "Do you remember how you came to be on the forest path?"

Anekah, with furrowed brows, replied, "I think I was looking for something, someone. It's all still foggy in my mind."

Ashima spoke with obvious concern, "What do you know about yourself?"

She looked to the corner of the ceiling, and opened her blouse, showing her birthmark. "I am called Anekah, for the brand I bear, where a necklace's pendant would be. The rest is still hazy."

"Family?" Ashima queried.

"I believe that only my dog and I survived the attack." She looked down at the ground.

The handmaid arrived with the bread and the wine.

Ashima exclaimed, "The attack, what attack?"

Anekah sighed deeply and held out a hand to Ashima, which she took. Anekah lifted her eyes heavenward, "Blessed are You, O King of the Universe, for supplying us with the fruit of the vine and the produce of the earth." She squeezed Ashima's hand as she let go, reached out, took a piece of bread in one hand and a goblet of wine in the other. Her next words were garbled as her mouth was full.

Ashima took a goblet herself, "I'm sorry, I couldn't understand what you said."

She smiled and swallowed, "My dog's name is Seph." She paused a minute, "Would it be possible to take a bath?"

"Yes," Ashima stammered, "I'm sorry, I should have thought of that," and over her shoulder, "Bella, please run a bath for our guest."

She took another small swallow of wine, "Thank you, mistress, and your name?"

Ashima continued to stammer, "I don't know what has happened to my manners. I am Ashima, and this is the home of Lahab, son of Methuselah."

Astonishment seemed to sweep across her face, "Methuselah, THE Methuselah?"

"Yes," Ashima chuckled. "I think there is only one."

She raised her hands to the heavens, "Then regardless of my troubles, I have been truly blessed."

It was Ashima's turn to be astonished, "You know of Methuselah?"

She lifted her voice heavenward,

"In this world of darkness
where evil holds such sway,
there are none who shine so bright
as Enoch and Methuselah."

Ashima stood mesmerized by both her voice and words, until her handmaid interrupted with, "My mistress, the bath is ready."

Ashima shook her head to dispel the final remnants of the song and held out her hand. Anekah stood, took it, and together they walked hand-in-hand to where the bath had been prepared. Anekah disrobed and took Ashima's hand again as she stepped into the steaming water that smelt intoxicatingly of roses. She sat, closed her eyes, and relished it all as she let go of Ashima's hand.

Ashima spoke softly, "I will leave you with Bella. She will see to your every need while I find you some suitable clothing."

She turned and left the room. Almost unnoticed, Seph had padded to the tub and placed his head on the rim. She shook her hand free of the water, reached out, and caressed his head.

Chapter Fourteen
A New Life Begins

Anekah whispered to Seph, "Well, what do you think?" He answered so only Anekah could hear, "I think that went well. What's next?"

"Right now? I think I will luxuriate in the tub for a bit."

His voice almost tinkled, "Don't fall back to sleep."

She sat a little taller in the water, "Okay," and scrubbed the grime out of her face, hair, and washed all over.

She was done when Ashima returned with her arms full of clothing. Bella lay down a towel for her to step out of the tub onto, held another to wrap around her, and then helped her into a clean set of clothing.

Bella addressed her, "Mistress Anekah, when we have finished dressing you, I have been charged with escorting you to the family dinner by way of my Master's study. It was he and his men who found you on the forest path."

Anekah wondered if she should be apprehensive, but decided that she would not be. If worse came to worse, she could just act tired and still somewhat confused. Which she still was.

Bella stoped at the entrance to the study and announced, "The young woman, Anekah, who you found on the forest path." She stepped back to allow Anekah to walk into the study, but Anekah paused at the door. This was the first good look she had at Lahab. He appeared to be old enough to be her grandfather. He was dressed well, but not ostentatiously. He sat at a writing desk, a roll of scrolls within reach to his right. He had been writing something as Bella spoke. He stopped, put his pen in the ink well, scooted his seat back, and stood up.

"Come in, my dear, and have a seat." He pointed to a seat on the other side of his desk. It was actually a seat, not the usual cushion. She looked at it, wondering at its strange design. "It's okay, it's just a chair, not a cushion. It seems easier to talk to one another face to face sitting on them this way," then he added, "If you don't mind."

She took her seat, "Okay."

He sat as well.

"How are you doing?" His voice was laced with concern.

She sighed, "Quite well, considering. The bath was wonderful, these clothes too."

"And your memory," he creased his brow.

She looked off into the distance, "That is still hazy. I know my name, partly because of the birthmark," and she touched her chest, "and Seph. He has always been with me." She looked to the doorway where the dog sat. "The rest," and she just shook her head.

"It will probably come back, in time. Are you okay to stay with us for awhile?" He didn't want to presume.

She returned her gaze to his eyes, "That would be very kind of you, taking in a young woman you found on a forest path."

A smile graced his face, "It will be our pleasure." He paused for a moment, "We are about to have dinner and some of my family are here. Would you feel up to eating with us and meeting with them?"

She broke eye contact again, "You are too kind."

His smile broadened, "Think nothing of it." He stood.

Bella had just entered the doorway, next to the dog, "Dinner?"

He still faced Anekah, "Do you think you could send your dog with Bella?"

A mischievous grin found its way to Anekah's face, but Lahab couldn't see it. She spoke commandingly, "Seph, go with Bella." Seph stood and followed Bella as she left.

Bella called over her shoulder, "I'll see that he's fed with our dogs."

Lahab reached out a hand, cupped, palm downward toward Anekah. She placed her palm on the back of his hand and he escorted her to dinner.

Chapter Fifteen
And What a Dinner

Together they walked into the dining hall.

"Family, I'd like to introduce you to Anekah. She will be staying with us for a time." He walked her to the head of the table and began to introduce his family, starting to his right, and moving counter-clock-wise: "This is my father Methuselah, my brother Lamech, his son Noah." He passed over an empty seat complete with place setting and goblet. "Then there are Noah's three sons: Shem, Ham, and Japheth." Anekah had been nodding at each of them as they were introduced. When Lahab got to Japheth and she looked at him, preparing to nod, their eyes locked and something seemed to pass between them, something almost prescient.

Both she and Japheth shuddered involuntarily. *"Surely no one else noticed that,"* she hoped, *"but what was that?"*

Lahab moved on past an empty setting and continued, "My other brother Abiel, and my sister Maliel." She nodded to his final two guests as Lahab gestured to the seat at his left.

She thought, *"Isn't that his wife's seat?"* Then she realized that Ashima's time would be consumed on serving her guests and seeing to their every need. She sat and noticed that Japheth still looked at her, bedazzled.

Lahab sat and motioned to Methuselah, "Father?"

Methuselah stood and spoke towards the empty seat, "Lord God, King of the Universe, we thank You for the food, for family, and for what You are doing though us as light in a dark world," and he sat.

Ashima and her servants brought out bread still warm from the oven and wine. This was followed by lamb and steaming vegetables.

Methuselah spoke again, with a lyric lilt to his voice, "Anekah, do you know the meaning of your name?"

She smiled at him, "I do, a branded necklace."

He continued, "and do you know why you're named that?"

She opened the front of her robe a little to show the small birthmark below her neck. "I do. I have been branded since birth to show that I belong to him," and she pointed upwards toward the ceiling, "Like you and your father in the midst of this crooked and perverse generation." She paused, "The righteousness of the world is in this room." She looked at the doorway, "What if the enemy were to strike a blow here tonight? He could destroy much of the future in a single stroke."

Methuselah looked at the doorway too, where Anekah's dog sat. "Much of our security and protection is not obvious to the naked eye." He laughed lightly, "You must have mesmerized my son for your dog to be allowed to sit there."

Anekah looked at the floor, "He's all I have left, so your son has made me a small concession," and she looked to Lahab.

Methuselah sighed, "Yes, one of his many endearing qualities. He reads people very quickly and very accurately." He reached for the carafe of wine, "May I pour you some wine?"

She held out her goblet to him, "Please."

He filled his own and then raised it, "To our future. May it continue to be secure, and may Anekah find her place in our family."

As he finished, Anekah looked again at Japheth. He met her gaze solidly and then he dipped his head slightly to acknowledge her gaze before he took another sip from his goblet. *"Well,"* she thought, *"at least he noticed I was looking at him."*

Anekah wasn't one much for small talk. She didn't seem to remember much of her life before the forest path, but she was a good listener. Maliel, Lahab's sister, seemed quite a remarkable woman in her own right. She had obviously won the right to sit at this table amongst the most powerful men in the country. She kept Anekah on the edge of her seat with the tales of her shrewd business dealings. In a culture filled with greed and dishonesty, it was interesting to note how humility and trust won favor even from the most corrupt. One of the questions asked often in the marketplace was, "Is this as strong a bond that accompanies the word of Maliel?" It was quite a compliment on the value all held of her word and promise.

After dinner they grabbed their goblets and retired to a large lounge area. Anekah sat on a cushion and by luck, providence, or design, Japheth sat next to her.

He began, "So, you remember little before Lahab found you collapsed in the forest?"

She sighed deeply, "Only fragments, like stories about Enoch and Methuselah, but about my family, upbringing, those things? I can recall very little. Perhaps the sound of my mother's voice, the safety of my father's arms, not much else."

Japheth smiled, he had a nice smile, "And about the dog?"

She returned his smile, "Yes, that he is my best friend and I can totally trust and rely on him."

He wrinkled his brows, "You speak of him as if he's almost human."

She looked wistfully away, "To me he is."

"That doesn't seem odd to you?"

She countered, "Not in the least. He likes you, by the way."

His smile returned, "Well, at least he has good taste," and he chuckled. He had a nice chuckle too. "So, what do you think you will be able to contribute to this family? You certainly don't look like a "free loader."

She scrunched up her face, "Hmm, a little early to tell. You don't know me very well yet and I don't know you, so...." and she left it hanging there.

"Would you like a quick tour before it gets too dark?" He ventured. She nodded, so he addressed his father, "Okay if I give Anekah a quick tour of our facilities?"

Noah looked to Lamech, who nodded, "Sure, but don't stray too far afield. As she has already noted, we do have many enemies."

She addressed Lamech, "Not to worry, Seph will be with us," and she looked to the doorway where the dog now stood.

Japheth held out his hand palm cupped downward towards her. As she stood up, she placed her hand on the top of his and they walked to the doorway.

Chapter Sixteen
Lahab's Land

Together Japheth and Anekah walked out of the lounging area and Seph joined them. Although she hadn't seen much of the house before, Japheth led her straight for the large entryway. He dropped her hand as they stopped at a closet for coats. He opened the door and they stepped out into the early twilight. The guard, Bedad, stood at the door.

Bedad turned around, "Master Japheth?"

"Bedad, Mistress Anekah and I," and then he added, "and her dog are going to tour the stables."

He responded, "Do you need a bodyguard?"

The dog growled and Japheth respond, "Nope, it looks like we'll be fine with just the dog."

As they began the journey to the stables, Anekah reached over and took his hand. Initially surprised, he willingly accepted it. A slight smile graced her face, but she was looking away at Seph, so he didn't see it. At the large stable door he let go of her hand to slide the large door on its track. The inside was well lit by glass chimney enclosed candle lights.

Anekah had preceeded him in and walked straight to one of the horse stalls.

It held a majestic black stallion who stood tall and snorted. She strode right up to the rail.

"Anekah," Japheth called out in alarm and stepped to stop her, but she beat him to the rail.

She held out a hand, over the rail, palm upward as she said, "Midnight, it's okay."

Japheth shook his head. *"How does she know his name?"* The horse himself looked stunned, then lowered his head and stepped forward. "He bites!" he nearly yelled.

Anekah ignored him and spoke to the horse, "It's okay," she soothed, "it's me." She spoke as if he knew her or at least as if she knew him. He lowered his head to sniff her hand, then lowered it more to let her softly run her cupped hand up the bridge of his nose. He sidestepped to the rail and she reached her other hand over it to scratch his neck as she rubbed his nose. He leaned against the rail, reveling in her touch.

Japheth stood there amazed. He knew this horse and never in all of his days had he seen him act like this to any person, ever. Anekah turned smiling, "I think I may be a bit of a 'horse whisperer.'" She patted his neck and moved on to repeat the performance at each succeeding stall. She pointed to the door they now approached, "And out there?"

It took a moment for him to find his voice, "The sheep pens."

She clasped her hands in glee, "Oh, goodie." She had the door open before he could stop her. As she stepped out of the doorway, a bow twanged. She plucked the arrow out of the air before it could reach her and turned towards Japheth to whisper, "You didn't see that. It was a trick of the light." He shook his head as if he had suddenly become befuddled and she let the arrow fall next to the stable wall. About one hundred cubits away there was some scuffle in the forest, followed by running feet, and then it was quiet again.

Seph trotted back from the forest to sit next to the sheepdog, Uzza. Anekah walked up to Uzza and knelt down to pet him. "What is the name of the lead ram," she asked Seph

"Dumah," the dog replied.

She gave Uzza a final ruffle, "and called out, "Dumah." A ram's head perked up and looked around. She called again, "Dumah, come," and gestured with her hand down towards her side. The ram walked towards the fence of the sheepfold, as Anekah knelt on one knee and reached through the fence. The ram didn't even sniff her hand, but just walked up to the fence and leaned against it so that Anekah could pet him. She looked up at Japheth, who still stood there dumbfounded. She shrugged her shoulders, "Maybe an animal whisperer, too," like it was no big deal. She gave him a final pat on the head and stood up. She addressed Japheth, "How many shepherds do you have?"

"Ah, six, I think," he stammered. He thought to himself, *"How did she know the lead ram's name?"*

"Is there space for another?" she asked.

"I'm not sure. I'll have to ask Lahab." He looked a tad concerned. "All the others will be male," he added.

She chuckled. "Not a problem, I have Seph," like that answered all of his questions. "Where is the armory?"

His stammer continued, "Ah….back towards the house."

"Can we go see it?"

He spread his hands, "Sure, why not."

The Armory was guarded, but the guard recognized Japheth,."Master Japheth, how may I help you?"

"Kaleph, this is Anekah, Lahab's new ward. We'd like a look around if that's okay?"

His smile was a little crooked, but he tried, "Sure, be my guest, but be careful. All the weapons are sharp."

Chapter Seventeen
Starting at the Armory

The guard opened the metal door. It was obviously well oiled as it did not creak or squeak when opened. The armory too was well lit. All of Lahab's property and possessions were well taken care of. There was armor, shields, swords, lances, and axes, all hanging on the walls. They sparkled as a testimony to their excellent condition. There was also a section of bows. Anekah walked up to them, selected one and took it off the wall.

She looked to Japheth, "I would like to borrow this for a bit." He wasn't sure he could be more surprised, but he was. "Who makes your bows?"

"Ah, the Master Woodworker." He was thinking his stammer was in danger of becoming permanent.

Her smile disarmed him again, "Let's go visit him."

"Ah, it just so happens, he usually works late. You better let me carry the bow out of the armory, though." She handed it to him and he walked to the doorway. "Kaleph, I'm going to borrow this bow."

"Certainly, Master. Arrows?" he asked.

He looked at Anekah, who shook her head, "Not right now thanks."

They walked to another building. The lights were on. Since it was just the Woodworker's workshop there was no need of a guard. Japheth knocked, then opened the door and allowed Anekah to go in.

He quickly followed her with a, "Melek, this is Lahab's new ward. I am showing her around his holdings and she asked to see you."

Melek had risen from his work table at the knock on his door. "How may I be of assistance to you, mistress?"

She held out her hand to Japheth, who place the bow in her hand. She smiled. Yes, that smile would melt the snow. "Master Melek, I was wondering if you could make me a bow?" He looked surprised to Japheth, who just shrugged his shoulders. She went on, "It would need to be about two-thirds this size."

Melek looked at Japheth again, who shrugged again. "And the 'pull-weight'?" he ventured.

With the bow in her right hand she pulled the string to her cheek, "About like this would be fine," and she handed the bow to him. He pulled the string to his own cheek, but not with the same level of effortlessness.

His eyes widened, "I see that you pulled the bow left-handed. Is that what you also desire, a left-handed bow?"

She bowed slightly, "Please."

He looked at Japheth, even more surprised. "I'll be right back." He left them, went into the back room, and returned with a short, left-handed bow. He had already strung it. "I have no idea why I made this the other day, but here it is."

Now her own eyes were wide with surprise. She took it from his hand, drew the string to her cheek, and pronounced, "It's perfect."

"Arrows?" he asked.

"About a dozen target arrows would be wonderful, not the broad heads you would use for a large animal." She confided in him.

Melek smiled, "I have those too. I'll go get them for you."

She stopped him, "Before you go. Have you ever made a flute?" It seemed a silly question.

He looked at her, brow furrowed, thinking, *"I don't believe this."* He turned and left without completing the thought. He returned with a dozen arrows in a left-hand quiver, a leather arm protector, and another small pouch about a span in length. She handed the bow to Japheth and put on the arm protector and quiver. She then took the pouch, opening it to reveal a small flute. She put it to her lips and played the first few measures of a light and lilting little melody. As the smile left his face. he asked, "You are not a sorceress, are you? A seer?"

She shook her head *"No."*

He went on, "How could you possible know I had prepared these things?"

"I only knew that I wanted them," she replied.

He sighed and looked up to the ceiling, "Well, now you have them."

To this she replied, "Thank you, I am truly grateful."

Anekah turned and headed for the door, quiver over one shoulder, flute and pouch over the other, and bow in hand.

Shaking his head, also in disbelief, Japheth followed her. They stopped by the armory to return the other bow. She waited outside and talked with Kaleph while Japheth went inside to rehang the bow on the wall. She offered her free hand to Japheth as he emerged from the armory, which he took, and they walked back to the palace together, holding hands.

He took her to her room and left her with, "Are you always that mysterious?" At which Seph yipped. Japheth had forgotten that the dog had accompanied them the entire evening. It was like the dog was saying, *"You haven't seen anything yet!"* They said their goodnights and she closed the door. He stood there a moment, reviewing the evening, shaking his head in disbelief. Then he heard her playing the pipe. It was beautiful and reminded him of a deep pink sunset.

Chapter Eighteen
Reporting to Lahab

Japheth went directly to Lahab's study to report. He had Bella announce him. "Master Lahab, Jepthah is here to see you," and she ushered him into the room.

Lahab called to her, "Could you bring us some wine please?"

Of course, she responded, "Yes, my lord, right away, my lord," and scurried off to fetch it.

Lahab sat at his desk, surrounded by parchments. "Well Jepthah, what do you think of her?"

He looked at the floor, "Permission to speak plainly, my lord."

"My lord, nothing! I'm your granduncle. You can always speak plainly when it is just the two of us." He spoke almost curtly.

"She is quite an enigma," he began. "She appears to be an animal whisperer, having a special connection to them all. She had Midnight eating out of her hand and the alpha ram came right over to the pen railing when she called him to be petted. We stopped by the armory and she had me bring her and a bow to the master woodworker where she proceeded to request a short bow and showed that she could handle one, left-handed. She had him eating out of her hand too. It was almost as if she were a seer. He had already prepared a short left-handed bow on a whim, complete with arrows and quiver. When she asked if he had ever carved a flute, I thought he would faint. He had just finished one of those too. He gave them all to her, which she received graciously. When I left her at her room she was playing the flute even before I had a chance to walk away. She plays it exquisitely. She asked about our shepherds and I got the feeling she would feel privileged if you asked her to become one."

Up until that point Lahab had just been nodding in agreement. When Jepthah mentioned her desire to become a shepherd, he balked. "But the shepherds are all male. Who would protect her sleeping with them out under the night sky?"

Japheth chuckled, "She said, 'I have Seph,' and he growled like he had been listening. I think this fascinating young woman can take care of herself. She was, after all, alone in the forest."

Lahab looked away, to the corner of the ceiling. "Hmmm, I truly wonder why she has been brought to us. Thank you, Japheth, for your care of her this evening. We have lots to think and pray about. I'll talk to her myself in the morning." Then, almost as if on cue, the mysterious sound of a faraway flute could be heard in the distance, "Good night, Japheth, and thank you again."

Japheth bowed slightly, "My pleasure," and he felt sure that Anekah would haunt both his thoughts and his dreams. He was correct. Her flute's soft music drifted lightly on the wind until he was fast asleep.

The next morning, after breakfast, Lahab asked Anekah to join him in his study. She sat again across from him, her hands comfortably folded in her lap.

He rested his elbows on his desk, and his chin in his hand, "Do you wonder why I have called you into my study?"

She smiled slightly. "Probably the result of my time with your grandnephew. He may feel I have bewitched him." She surmised.

His smile was larger, "You are correct. He says you have a special connection with animals."

She nodded, "I do."

"Are you any good with the bow you were given last night? I know you are with the flute, that was quite a beautiful last hour of the evening." He asked and concluded.

She blushed, "I have not tried the bow yet. Do you have a target area I could practice at?"

"I do. Would you like to try it?"

"I would. I seem to remember using one, but it is unconfirmed as yet."

He continued, "Would it be all right if Japheth accompany you again? Do you get along okay?"

She blushed again, "Yes, and yes."

"He also mentioned something about your desire to become one of my shepherds." He scowled. "Would you be safe out all night with my shepherds? They are all male."

She met his gaze directly, "I have Seph."

That was certainly her answer, just as Japheth had said. "Fine, I'll have him take you to the practice field and we can talk again this afternoon." She began to get up, but his voice stopped her, "Anekah, we are quite glad that we found you along that forest path."

She bowed slightly, "Me too," then turned and left his presence.

Chapter Nineteen
Lahab's Practice Field

Japheth knocked on the door of what had become Anekah's room. He even had brought a bow and quiver full of arrows for himself. As she answered the door, he asked her, "Do you ride horses? We need to ride to the practice field."

She smiled and he realized that she had dimples, "Yes, I do." Then she added, "Can I ride Midnight? I think we have a special connection."

Japheth shook his head, "I had one of the mares saddled, but I guess I could remedy that and have Midnight saddled if you prefer."

"No, that's okay, a mare will be fine." Then she laughed, "This time." She stepped out of her room, bow in hand, quiver over her shoulder, and took his other hand as she walked by. She almost skipped.

The mare was a beautiful bay. Anekah walked up to it, let it sniff her hand, and petted the side of her nose. The mare stepped in close and nuzzled Anekah. "I think she likes me, this should be fun." She practically leapt into the saddle.

Once again Japheth just stood there with his mouth open. Then he mounted his own black stallion. It wasn't Midnight, but still an impressive steed. He led the way to the practice field by half a length. She and her mare were just off the stallion's shoulder. There was a guard at the gate to the field, probably just for security. They dismounted, dropped their reigns over a nearby tree limb, and walked into the field, bows in hand.

She wondered how they kept the field's green grass cropped so short. The field was about a stadia wide and five stadia long. They laid their bows on the grass and walked to the side of the field where three hay bales lay. They each picked up one. Japheth was surprised that Anekah could easily lift one. *"Would she always be surprising him?"* They walked to the center of the field's width and he set his down. She set hers on top of his. While he went back for the third one, she walked thirty-five paces back towards their bows, took an arrow from her quiver and stuck it in the ground. She then went back to retrieve both their bows and meet Japheth where she had placed the arrow.

"Thirty-five paces," and she handed him his bow.

Because she was left-handed and he was right-handed, they could face each other as they shot. He had also produced a two cubit square target from someplace and attached it to the bales while he was there.

"Ladies first," he offered. The center of the target was a red circle a span in diameter. She nocked an arrow and drew the end of the arrow and string slowly and steadily to her cheek. She slowly exhaled and before she took the next breath let the arrow fly. The target responded with a loud *"Thwap!"* Her arrow now stood in the very center of the target. She had wondered if she should pull the first arrow a little off center, but in the end decided, *"He's going to have to learn to accept me for who I am."*

He looked at the target, to her, back to the target, "Thought you'd set the bar a little high, eh?"

She shrugged. He nocked his own arrow, pulled it back, and let it fly. It was a hand span to the left and high of hers in the center. She smiled.

She thought to herself, *"I have never split an arrow before. Naw, they are too expensive."*

She put her second arrow a finger's width to the right of her first. Japheth scowled and put his next arrow halfway between his first one and her first one. She nodded to him and put her next one a finger's width to the left of her first. His next shot was between his first two, hers a finger width above her first. He must have been frustrated as he pulled his next two arrows a full span to the left. Her final arrow was a finger's width below her first. All five arrows were within a three finger circle of the target's center.

Just as Japheth released his fifth arrow, Seph yipped. He was looking off to the edge of the field. A young lion walked out of the forest.

Japheth quickly nocked another arrow, but Anekah whispered, "Wait!"

The young lion was followed by a full-size lion. Anekah recognized them both, but Japheth did not know that. She stepped left between Japheth and the lions.

He whispered loudly, "What are you doing," and took a step to her right.

Anticipating him, she also stepped to the right, placing herself between him and the lions again. She held up her hand and began to slowly walk forward as she quietly says, "I am an animal whisperer, remember."

He responded, "Horses and sheep are one thing, but lions?"

Looking at the back of her head he saw her nod, bend over to lay her bow on the ground, and continue walking.

The dog joined her and they walked towards the lions together. The lions sat and the adult roared. Japheth pulled the arrow string to his cheek only to realize that he only had target arrows. Even if he were able to squeak one by Anekah, he would only wound one of the lions. Both would attack and it would be all over. He relaxed the string, fell to his knees and began to fervently pray in a whisper, "Please, please, please…"

Anekah held her hand out for the adult lion to sniff. Her dog sat in front of the younger lion. She caressed the lion's nose, then stepped to hug him around the neck and scratch him behind the ear. She looked back to Japheth.

His forehead is touched the ground as he softly pounded the earth in earnest supplication.

She called out lightly. "Everything is okay, but you had probably better stay there as the lion does not know your intentions." She laughed lightly to herself.

Kilyah spoke, but of course Japheth could not hear them, "How are things?"

She sighed, "Being knocked unconscious was difficult, but I am okay now. I have been accepted as Lahab's ward and will most likely become a shepherd to earn my keep."

"That could be good," but he added, "but you will still need to be careful. We can try and help keep predators away, but you have to remember we are new here and our presence not yet fully established. We will share your goodness with as many as we can, but there will still be renegades."

She kneaded his mane, "Understood, thanks for your help."

He bowed slightly, "Our pleasure, Anekah. I will give one more roar and then leave before your friend faints." He did roar and then padded back into the jungle, along with the younger lion.

She turned and walked back to Japheth, picking up her bow along the way. Seph followed her.

Japheth struggled up from his knees, "How did you know that you wouldn't be eaten alive?"

"I can usually tell. It's part of the gift. Let's retrieve our arrows. That's probably enough excitement for one afternoon." He heartily agreed.

Chapter Twenty
Japheth's Report

Japheth left Anekah at the stable and went straight to his granduncle. She would want to spend time with each of the horses anyway.

Bella announced him at the study entrance, "Japheth, my lord."

He looked up from his scrolls, "Ah, Japheth, how was the target practice?"

"She put five arrows right in the center of the target, all within a finger-width of each other." He paused and took a breath, "And if that wasn't enough, two lions came out of the forest, an adult and a younger one, and she proceeded to walk up and pet them. She's not just an animal whisperer, but fearless too."

Lahab scratched his chin thoughtfully, "I guess she'll make a decent shepherdess then. Have the six of them and her meet me in here after dinner." He smiled at Japheth, "You like her don't you?"

"What?" he stammered.

His smile lingered, "You may not have admitted it to yourself yet, but I think you are a bit star-struck."

He pretended to challenge it, "No I'm not."

"I think my friend, you protest too strongly, and give yourself away."

He turned to go, "I'll let the shepherds know that you want to meet with them, and her." He stomped out. He turned the corner and stopped, *"Do I like her? Admire, yes, but like?"* He tried to dismiss it, but to no avail. His granduncle's words continued to interrupt his thoughts. He stomped his foot, that helped. Then he headed to speak with the shepherds.

Japheth enter the shepherds' quarters to find them lounging around a table, telling stories. They stopped when they saw him. One of them pompously asked, "How can we help you Master Japheth?" The others chuckled.

"Lahab wants to speak with you in his study after dinner." That sobered them up.

Their spokesman, Balek, continued, "Do you happen to know the reason why?"

Now it was his turn to appear pompous, "Your master, wants his new ward, Mistress Anekah, to join you tonight as a new shepherdess."

Balek laughed, "You've got to be kidding." Suddenly, he winked at the others, "This could... prove interesting."

Japheth laughed back at them, "And her dog will eat any one of you that even looks at her sideways." He turned and left their presence, still laughing under his breath. *"They have no idea what surprises their evening holds for them,"* he thought to himself.

After dinner, Japheth, Anekah, and the six shepherds gathered in Lahab's study. "Did Japheth confide in you the reason for this little meeting?"

Balek answered for the shepherds, "He said that you might want your new ward, Mistress Anekah, to join us tonight as we go out with the sheep." He looked at his fellow shepherds, "I must admit that I have some difficulty with that decision, Master Lahab."

Lahab looked at him until he looked away, "You would question my decision?"

Looking at the ground, Balek responded, "No, my lord."

Lahab went on, "Are you worried about her safety?" Balek shook his head. "Have you been told about her dog?" He nodded. "Good, then it's settled. Take her out with you tonight. That is all." They all got up to leave.

Anekah spoke to Balek as she left, "I will go to my room and change and then I will be right over."

Chapter Twenty-One
Behold the Shepherdess

When Anekah entered the shepherds' quarters she was dressed like all the rest of them. If they hadn't known she was a woman they wouldn't have been able to tell. She wore her quiver and her bow on her back.

Balek handed her a staff, "We haven't been formally introduced, Mistress."

Anekah quickly replied, "You do not need to call me Mistress. When we are together, I am just one of you."

Balek relaxed, "Good." He went around the circle, "This is Bohan, Allon, Eder, Jashon, and Tartak." She nodded to each of them as they were introduced and they nodded back. "Did you bring a bedroll?"

She sighed, "No, but I plan to stay awake the entire time as this is my first evening." She gestured behind her, "This is Seph. I must warn you, for your own good, that he is fiercely protective of me. Whose dog is Uzza?"

Balek furrowed his brows, "How do you know my dog's name?"

She replied nonchalantly, "We met while Japheth was showing me the sheep," like that was all the answer needed. "And how are the sheep divided among you?"

Allon spoke up, "We each have about one sixth of the sheep that follow us."

She addressed Balek, "Do you have Dumah too?"

He was starting to think she might be a witch. "You know my lead ram's name too?"

She just smiled, "Yes, I happen to know that too." She paused, "Since I probably need to prove myself before any sheep are assigned to me," and she looked directly at Balek, "Could I just sort of tag along with you tonight?"

The others all smiled behind their hands as Balek responded, "Ah....sure." Then he asked, "Are you any good with that bow? It seems a little short."

She smiled, "I am," she paused slightly, "A longer one would tend to get in the way, plus I have the staff if I need it. Thank you for lending it to me."

He looked sternly at her, "Consider it yours," then he added, "Assuming this shepherding thing works out for you."

At the sheepfold Anekah walked up to the gate and called out, "Dumah," to which the lead ram responded and walked over to her at the gate. She reached over to scratch it between the horns and then bent over to caress its neck. Balek thought, *"Yup, she knows my lead ram."* Bohan stepped to the gate, opened it, and called his sheep forth. About one sixth of them responded and walked out of the pen to follow him. Next, it was Allon's turn. Each shepherd did the same, until all that remained was Balek, Anekah, Dumah and the rest of Balek's sheep. He called them and they followed the three of them.

They had all the sheep bedded down and Allon had built a fire when Balek and Anekah left to take the first watch. They sat beneath an oak, with their backs to it. Anekah had her flute out and was playing a slow soft melody that reminded Balek of a sunset, when suddenly Seph began to growl.

"What is it, boy?" She whispered.

"Lion," he responded, but of course Balek couldn't understand him. She dropped the flute as she leapt to her feet, grabbing the bow, and then nocking an arrow. She whispered, "Lion!"

He thought, *"How could she know that?"*

She responded to his unasked question, "Part of the gift," as if that explained everything. She stepped forward and he tried to restrain her as he too stood, but he missed. In the moonlight, about sixty cubits away stood one of the lambs, a lion silently stalking it. She began walking towards the duo.

After a few paces she stopped, bringing her bow into position and saying, "It would be in your best interest to turn around and leave my lamb alone."

To Balek it sounded like the lion growled back, but Anekah heard, "I have heard of you. 'The Whisperer,' humph. I will not do what you ask. Rather, I will kill and eat as I please." He prepared to pounce, only to receive an arrow right through the temple, and fall dead to the ground.

Balek stood there astounded as she walked over to the lion and muttered, "You had your chance."

She hung her bow over her shoulder and with some difficulty removed the arrow from the lion's skull. It wasn't a broad head, but a field pointed practice arrow. She wiped the blood and brains off the arrow in the lion's mane, placed it in the quiver, then handed the quiver and bow to Balek who now stood beside her. She then went over and picked up the still shaking lamb, placed it around her neck and shoulders as she softly talked to it. She looked back at Balek and nodded towards their encampment. He walked back with her, still astounded at what he had just witnessed. She stooped to pick up her pipe along the way and Seph followed them both back to the fire.

The others were asleep as she sat the lamb down, sat herself down and then scooped the lamb into her lap before the fire, "Give me a few minutes to get the lamb settled and then I will rejoin you on watch. The dead lion may attract other predators that may need to also be discouraged.

Balek nodded, set down her bow and quiver, and went back out to the watch place they had established. Interestingly, Seph followed with him, just in case.

Chapter Twenty-Two
The Tale Begins

That morning, after the sheep had time to graze, the other shepherds woke Anekah and Balek. Over breakfast they asked about the dead lion. Balek took a deep breath, "Seph alerted us with his growling. The lion was stalking one of our lambs. Anekah told it to leave, but it didn't listen, so, she shot it through the temple from almost sixty cubits, with a target arrow no less."

They all stood there, dumb-founded. Bohan finally responded, "One shot, from sixty cubits?"

They looked at her.

Anekah sighed deeply, "He was about to pounce on our lamb. I had no choice."

Allon voiced his concern, "And if you missed?"

She looked at the ground, "Things could have gotten pretty messy. Thankfully, I did not miss."

Tartak spoke with obvious awe, "Can you teach me to shoot like that?"

She looked him directly in the eye, "You would learn from a woman?"

He held her gaze, "I would learn from an expert, yes!"

She responded, "It will take time, commitment, and practice, but yes, I could teach you."

He bowed slightly to her.

It was Eder's turn to ask a question, "Should we get the sheep back to their pens until the lion carcass is gone?" They all nodded and led their flocks out of the hills.

Balek stood before Laban. All the other shepherds including Anekah stood behind him as he described the events of the previous night. Anekah looked at the floor. She was embarrassed by the attention. Balek explained, "She was playing her flute softly when Seph began to growl," which he did now as Balek told the story.

Lahab looked at the dog and smiled, "Continue."

"She dropped the flute and in one fluid motion leapt to her feet, picking up her bow. Before I could blink, she had nocked an arrow and stepped forward, proclaiming, 'Lion, leave the lamb alone.' She was already beyond my grasp it seemed the lion refused as it was preparing to pounce when she shot it through the temple. It dropped dead on the spot. She handed me the bow, went forward, retrieved the arrow, cleaned it on the lion's mane, put it in her quiver and handed me that too. Then she picked up the still trembling lamb, put it on her shoulders and we went back to the others." He had said that almost in a single sentence. He took a deep breath, "I am in favor of letting her join us on a permanent basis."

Lahab turned to Anekah, "What do you have to say for yourself?"

She looked back down at the floor, "I was just doing my job?" But a smile was slowly forming at the corners of her mouth.

Lahab then asked, "Do you still want to become one of my shepherds?"

She looked up, "Killing the lion was difficult, protecting your sheep was not. Yes, I would still like to become one of your shepherds."

He turned to the other shepherds, "Because she is my ward she will have to sleep up here at the house, rather than with the rest of you. Can you all live with that?" They all nodded, nearly in unison. "Then it's settled." He called out, "Bella, give them an extra jug of wine to celebrate their newly appointed member."

She stuck her head in the doorway, "Yes, my lord," and went off to fetch it.

They waited outside the study doorway for Bella to return and then they all went back to the shepherds' quarters to celebrate.

Balek addressed Eder before them all, "What has been the greatest threat to our flock that you have faced?"

Eder thought a minute, "Well, the greatest threat was probably the same lion that Anekah killed last night, but I never faced it. It always got in, stole a lamb, and departed. She, however, caught it in the act and killed it. Let's hear it for Anekah," and he raised his glass.

They all raised their glasses and cheered.

Again, she looked at the floor embarrassed. "I'm sure if Seph had alerted you as he did me last night you would have done the same."

Allon spoke up, "I don't think any of us could have hit it at thirty cubits, let alone sixty." He raised his glass again, "To a great shot."

They again raised their glasses and cheered.

There was a knock at the door. Japheth opened it, and stepped in grinning, "What's all the ruckus about?"

Eder piped up, "Last night Anekah killed a lion and saved a lamb."

Japheth looked at her, but she was staring at the floor again, "Wasn't that dangerous?"

Balek puffed out his chest, "I was with her," then continued, "but not much help in the situation. She killed the lion with a single arrow to the temple, before it could pounce on the lamb."

She looked up at Japheth as he said, "Really? She is quite a shot. I can vouch for that."

Tartak added, "We can all vouch for that now. We have seen the lion," and he handed Japheth a full goblet of wine. "To easily the best archer among us," then he laughed, "but not the best shepherd, yet. It was, after all, only her first day."

Anekah added, "But what a day!" and they all laughed and took another pull from their goblets.

"Can I borrow her for a few minutes?" Japheth asked them.

They nodded their approval and he gestured towards the door. Japheth and Anekah took their goblets with them. He motioned to the front porch bench and she took a seat. He sat beside her,

"Quite a bit of excitement for your first evening of shepherding."

She shrugged her shoulders.

He raised his goblet, "Here's to a much quieter rest of the week."

She touched goblets with him and took a drink.

He paused and a look of seriousness came over him. "My father has some big announcement for the family supper this Friday evening. He won't tell any of us what it's about, but it seems rather grave."

Trying to lighten the mood she joked, "Your mother's pregnant?"

He smiled, "That would not be grave news except for her age, maybe." He reached over to take her hand, "Is it too soon for us to hold hands?"

They had held hands before when walking, but she pulled her hand away now. "It depends on your meaning. What are your intentions?" Now she was speaking gravely.

He didn't know if she was joking. Rather, he was more startled. He stammered, Ah....I....didn't....mean...anything by it."

She laughed, showing that she had been joking. "Then it is definitely too early." She waited a minute and then reached over and took his hand, "or does it mean that you like me?"

He held her hand and her gaze, "Like, admire, am in awe of, confused by, and much more."

She squeezed his hand, "Okay, but you may want to have a conversation with your father about us, to see if he approves. Since he doesn't know me like you do?"

Now it was his turn to look down at the porch deck, "Hmmm, yeah, I'll have to do that."

The rest of the week was thankfully uneventful.

Part Two
The End of the World

Chapter Twenty-Three
Just Another Family Dinner

Lahab stood at the head of the table, "Oh Lord, our God, King of the Universe, We thank you for all of this," and he gestured to include all the food on the table, "and for the fruit of the vine," and he held up his glass, "May all that we say and do tonight bring delight to your great heart," and he sat down. They were sitting around the table in pretty much the same order that they did every Friday evening.

After a wonderful meal and some great conversation, Noah stood up, "Earlier this week I went out to sit on a bench with Naamah in the middle of the forest of trees that we planted over twenty-five years ago. There was someone already there when we got there, Raych. Before I could even be shocked, He spoke and every fiber of my being resonated with his words. 'Noah, you have found favor in my sight. You are about to embark on the greatest adventure of your life.' If it was to be such a great adventure, I wondered why He seemed so solemn. He continued, 'I wanted you to know that I have determined to make an end of all flesh. The earth is filled with violence and corruption through out. Therefore, I will destroy all flesh from the face of the earth. I am bringing a flood of waters upon the earth to destroy all flesh in which is the breath of life. Everything that is on the earth shall die.' He said He was bringing a flood of waters. I did not understand what that meant, nor how He would do it, but He went on, 'I want you to build an ark of gopherwood.' Again I thought, 'Gopherwood? Wood from the gopher tree? The ones I planted over twenty-five years ago with my future wife in a plot of ground Tubal-Cain gave us?' Anyway, He just went on to describe the ark, its size, its interiors, and how to make it watertight. I'm guessing that it is going to float through this flood and we will be saved by being in it, me, my sons, and our wives. We will also be bringing a male and female of every kind of animal, bird, and creeping thing, along with the food they will need for the duration of the flood. Then He was gone and I was alone once again." He sat down. They were all in shock.

Finally Methuselah spoke up, "What did he say about me?"

Noah looked at the table, "I wondered about that and as I pondered this week, I was reminded that the loose translation of your name is, 'When he is gone it will come.' I think this 'flood' is the 'it' and you will be gone. I don't know if God will just 'take you' like he did your father or if you will die, but you will be gone when it comes."

Lamech spoke next, "And me?"

Noah took a slow deep breath, "I assume it will be the same with all of you, father. The only people on the ark will be me and my family." They all looked at one another.

Lamech also asked, "and the gopherwood?"

Noah chuckled, "Over twenty-five years ago, Naamah and I planted a grove of trees in a plot of ground that Tubal-Cain gave us before we were married. It is now a pretty nice forest."

Methuselah spoke again, "And when will this flood occur?"

Noah smiled, "Not as long as you are alive," and he paused, "nor until I design and build the means to process the lumber, and build an ark three hundred cubits in length."

Methuselah was still shaking his head, "And how on earth are you going to get two of every kind of animal to come into this ark?"

Noah laughed, "I have absolutely no idea."

Anekah looked at Japheth and their eyes met. Then she looked away to where they always left an empty place setting for "the stranger," if he should show up. She thought to herself, *"I think I have just found my destiny, or at least a piece of it."*

Chapter Twenty-Four
Just an Animal Whisperer?

Anekah and Japheth sat on the porch. He was not holding her hand at this point. He was confused and voiced his concern, "The end of all living things….."

She sighed, then interjected, "Except your family and all the animals that will be on the ark."

He snorted, "Yeah, all the animals, and how are we going to accomplish that?" He looked out into the dark.

She sighed again, "Japheth, I need to tell you something." He looked back at her. "I am more than an animal whisperer. I can actually communicate with them."

"Right!" he exclaimed in disbelief.

"I can prove it to you. Let's go to the stables." She held his gaze.

He got up, "Okay, show me!"

She held out her hand. He looked at it for a minute. Then his face softened and he took her hand.

They walked hand in hand to the stables. He was actually smiling again, a little. After closing the stable door behind them, Anekah dropped his hand and walked right up to Midnight's stable again.

Midnight walked over to her and nuzzled her. She hugged him and whispered in his ear, "Does Japheth know how you came to be here at Lahab's?" He nodded. "Since there is no way that I could know that too, tell me yourself."

He did.

With a hand still on Midnight's neck she spoke to Japheth, "Is there any way that I could know how Midnight came to be here? No, there is not, except that he just told me." She paused, "He was found in the wild, standing next to his mother who had stepped in a hole and broken her leg. His mother was shot and he was forcibly brought here as an orphan."

Japheth stood there with his mouth open.

"I would add, that I think the trauma of her death is partly responsible for his seemingly rebellious behavior."

Still in shock, Japheth asked, "How could you know that?"

"Like I just said, he told me."

"One of the grooms must have told you," he blurted out.

She sighed, "Then ask me something that only the two of you could know."

He looked at Midnight. "The first time he allowed me to ride him, what did I promise him?"

Anekah leaned her head against Midnight's neck, "You told him that you would make sure that he was always taken care of, to the end of his days."

"What?" he exclaimed, "That's not possible."

She patted his neck, "It is if we can communicate. Do you want me to go talk to your head sheepdog?"

Japheth scowled, still unconvinced, "Yes."

She gave Midnight one more hug, then walked over to Japheth and offered him her hand again. He looked down at it like he might be afraid to touch it, but took her hand anyway. They went out the other end of the stables where the sheep pens were. The head sheepdog, Uzza, was lying in front of the sheep gate. His head went up as they emerged, as did his ears.

Anekah spoke barely above a whisper, "It's okay, Uzza, it's just Japheth and I." His tail began to wag. She looked at Japheth, "What would you like me to ask him?"

He frowned, "What happened to his mother?"

She knelt down beside the dog and put her arm around his neck. Her eyes teared up, "While he was being trained by you and by her, he says his mother was attacked by a lion and carried away screaming. You were unable to bring the lion down, although you shot two arrows at him." She continued caressing the dog until his tail began to wag again and his ears came back up. Anekah wiped her eyes on her sleeve.

Japheth knelt down on the other side of the dog and put his arm around him too. Japheth whispered, "She can really communicate with you?"

Uzza lifted his head to look into Japheth's eyes and yipped.

Japheth looked into Anekah's eyes and said solemnly, "Okay, I believe you, but I don't think we should tell anybody else. At least not right now. Is that okay?"

Anekah gave him a faint nod.

Chapter Twenty-Five
The Questions

They both gave the dog a final hug and stood up. He offered her his hand and she took it. They walked slowly back to the porch and sat on the bench. Japheth looked down at the porch, "So, how are *you* going to survive the flood?"

Anekah smiled, "I think that should be pretty apparent."
He looked up at her, "You ask me to be your wife."

His eyes widened and he looked back down at the porch. "You're kidding."

She let go of his hand, lifted his chin, and looked directly in his eyes as she said, "Do I look like I'm kidding?"

Japheth took a breath and muttered, "Will you be my wife?"

Now she looked down at the porch, "Can I think about it?" She paused another moment, "No, now I'm kidding. Yes, I will be your wife!" She snickered, "We'll see if you can tame another wild horse."

He just shook his head, then asked, "Where is Seph, he is usually by your side, but I haven't seen him since supper."

She just shrugged, "He is a dog, you know. He's probably off doing his doggie business."

Shamah sat at their favorite refreshment table, eating a purple fruit and sipping from a goblet of wine. A portal opened and Rayeh stepped through. Shamah had poured him a goblet of wine which he picked up.

Rayeh asked, "So, what do you think?"

Shamah was almost afraid to respond. He gulped, "So, You are going to destroy all flesh?"

Rayeh looked off over his head, "Yes, it has gotten that bad. I will start over with the righteous branch of Noah's family."

Shamah seemed puzzled, "What about Anekah?"

Rayeh smiled, "Oh, you just missed it. Japheth asked her the same question. Her answer was simple, 'Make me your wife,' and then I can accompany you on the ark."

Shamah was now puzzled, "She said that?"

"Yes," Rayeh still smiled, "and he asked her and she accepted."

"But she is one of the Ashareem. How will they have any children?" he asked.

Rayeh took a slow deep breath himself. "Just as there was never a female Ashareem until Lucifer's and Haniel's, perhaps there has never been a fertile Ashareem until Anekah."

Shamah looked deep into the contents of his goblet as he wondered aloud, "I guess that's possible."

Rayeh chuckled, "You do remember to whom it is that you are speaking?"

Shamah blushed in embarrassment and gulped, "Ah… yes…I do."

A portal opened and R'gal walked through, "Shamah, what a privilege."

Although shocked, Shamah responded, "The privilege is mine."

R'gal laughed, "We could wrestle for the right to call it our privilege?"

Shamah laughed in return, "No, that's okay. I will defer to you and your privilege."

R'gal sighed, perhaps in relief at not having to wrestle with Shamah. "You have met Noah?"

Shamah relaxed too, "Yes, but I am more acquainted with his son Japheth."

R'gal went on, "I now serve Noah in my human form."

Shamah looked hopefully at Rayeh who added, "Perhaps after the wedding. Although, it usually takes nearly a year to prepare a home for the bride." Shamah looked down at the table, pretending he was disappointed, but he really knew that he couldn't fool Rayeh. "Then you will transition into R'gal's brother."

"*Ah*," thought Shamah, "*hope.*"

"And," Rayeh added, "perhaps you will come with some carpentry skills?" He looked at them both, "or others?"

Shamah frowned, "And how will I get those?"

Rayeh, however smiled, "I have a few ideas."

Shamah rolled his eyes, "Oh goodie, I can just imagine." Then he laughed. They all laughed.

Anekah had been ushered into Lahab's study. He motioned for her to sit in the chair on the other side of his desk. He was surprised at how relaxed she appeared.

"Japheth tells me that he wants to marry you." He said somewhat sternly, "Why would I allow him to do that, I hardly know you?"

She smiled, "You don't think that he loves me?"

"What has love got to do with it?" he said briskly.

"Perhaps I am a sorceress and have bewitched him?" she said curtly.

He shook his head, "No, I would know if that were the case."

She chuckled under her breath, "Not if I had bewitched you too."

He furrowed his brows and his eyes darted back and forth. *"Is that possible?"* he thought.

She chuckled, now, out loud, "No. I am not a sorceress and I have not bewitched either of you. May I speak plainly?"

He regained his composure, took a breath, and responded, "Yes, please do."

She began, "My coming here is no accident. I believe that I have been sent to you for a specific purpose."

He looked at her a little sideways, "And what is that purpose?"

She took a deep breath, "When the ark is ready, Noah is going to have to bring all of the animals into the ark. How is he going to do that? He has no idea and neither do you."

He sat back in his chair, putting his folded hands to his lips, "Go on."

"I have a gift. I can communicate with the animals." There, she had come right out and told him.

He was obviously skeptical, "Sure you can."

At that moment, a swallow lit on the window sill of the window in his study, "Why is that swallow sitting there?" and she pointed. He shrugged and she smiled, "I'll ask him." She got up, walked to the window, and uncharacteristically the swallow just sat there. Anekah spoke to the swallow, "Mister Swallow," she was interrupted. "Oh, your name is Soos. Why are you sitting on Lahab's window sill?" She waited, then turned back to Lahab. "He's here to thank you. It seems you have instructed your threshers not to sweep all the grain off the threshing floor, but to leave some grain for the birds. He says, 'Thank you.'"

Lahab sat there with his mouth open. Tears began to fill his eyes. He had indeed told his threshers that very thing, to leave some wheat for the birds, but he never thought one of the birds would come to his window to thank him. He asked, "How was he going to thank me if you were not here?"

She laughed lightly, "He just did."

"But that was only possible because you were here." A tear trickled down his cheek.

"Actually, Soos and I have met before. He heard that you had asked me to come see you tonight and thought this might be the right time. It seems that it was."

Lahab went on, "And you can talk to any and all animals?"

She looked over his head, "So far I haven't met any that I cannot talk to."

"And when the time is right, you think you can orchestrate their coming to the ark."

She took a deep breath, "I do."

He wiped his eyes, "Then I would be more than happy to have you marry Japheth. I will talk to Noah."

She grinned.

Chapter Twenty-Six
A Family Wedding

B ecause everyone felt a sense of urgency to build the lumber mill to produce the ark materials from Noah's gopherwood trees. Almost a year passed before they were able to complete everything required for the wedding. It would just be a family wedding, as they didn't really want the rest of the world to know that much about them and their family. They grew and raised everything that they needed, so there wasn't really any requirement for contact, other than that they cared about people. They would take seasonal products to the market that were beyond their needs. However, even with those contacts most people saw them as a bit odd.

Both of Japheth's brothers were also in relationships that would probably lead to marriage, but they were all within the extended family. Anekah was the only outsider, but then every one recognized that she was special, even those who did not know she could communicate with animals. She had kept her promise to Tartak and he was now a better archer than any of the others, save Anekah herself.

The ceremony itself was performed in the natural grove amidst the field of gopherwood trees that Noah and Naamah had planted years ago. It was a small, intimate family affair. The couple knelt at the very bench where Noah had proposed to Naamah. There, they made their promises to one another and exchanged gifts. Japheth gave her a bracelet of hammered gold that Tubal-cain had made for him. It contained a single gem, under which lay a hinge that covered a clasp to secure it around her wrist. She gave him the arrow head from the shaft she had used when she killed the lion that was about to pounce on Lahab's lamb. It hung on a gold chain that Tubal-cain had made for her, in exchange for some information that she had gathered from one of her animal friends. Of course, Tubal-Cain did not know the source of the information, but only that it had been extremely useful.

The couple spent a week together before the two of them returned to the fullness of public life, now as a couple. Seph had asked for a leave off absence from protecting her during the time the couple spent alone together. The small house that Japheth and his brothers had built for them was of gopherwood, like the ark would be. It was the first lumber, of that kind, their mill had produce to make sure that their process would actually work. It did work and it was their own version of wonderful. They called it the little ark. She was glad that they didn't need to test the "cover it with pitch, inside and out" requirement that would be applied to the ark.

Shamah sat at their favorite refreshment table. His thoughts were in such a turmoil that he wasn't eating and barely drinking. A portal opened and he was so lost in his thoughts that he didn't even notice.

"Ahem," Rayeh cleared his throat.

Shamah looked up, startled, "I'm sorry, Lord. I didn't notice your entrance."

A rather fit, mature man stood at Rayeh's side, "Let me present to you the latest incarnation of R'gal. His name is now Regem and he works for Noah."

Shamah squinted, "R'gal, that's really you?"

R'gal chuckled, "As I live and breathe."

Shamah shook his head to dispel the clouds, "And as you said before, you work for Noah?"

R'gal's smile grew, "Yes, I'm helping him design everything according to the plans, well at least the outline of the plan, that Rayeh gave him. What about you?"

Shamah sighed, "Well, Seph can't very well be lying at the feet of the newlyweds' bed, so, I asked for some leave and have been here."

R'gal looked at Rayeh, who nodded. "Are you ready to be my younger brother, Sirion?"

Shamah looked at Rayeh too, who nodded again. "Sure."

Regem entered Noah's study accompanied by Sirion.

"My lord, I would like to introduce my younger brother, Sirion, to you. I was thinking he could help Japheth run the wood mill. He is good with both machines and animals."

Noah looked at Sirion. "So, are you really good with animals and machines?"

Sirion replied humbly, "My lord, not as good as the renowned Tubal-Cain is with machines, nor as good as Anekah with animals, but in both cases pretty good and always willing to learn more."

Noah was impressed with both his words and demeanor, "Okay, Regem, take him to meet Japheth and Anekah."

They left Noah and walked to the small home of Japheth and Anekah. The entire compound of Noah and his family was well protected. There was no need for soldiers at each home. They knocked, and waited on the porch. Anekah answered.

Regem introduced his brother, "Mistress, this is my brother, Sirion."

Anekah looked at him quizzically. He looked somehow familiar.

Regem continued, "You have met him before."

"No, I don't believe that I have." She was pretty sure she had never met him, just that he seemed familiar.

Regem smiled, "Didn't you grow up with a dog named, Seph?" A tear filled her eye and she nodded. He gestured towards his brother. "That's why he seems so familiar."

She gasped, then stepped forward to embrace him, "Seph? I can't believe that you're back."

At that moment, Japheth stepped into the doorway and saw the two embracing, "Excuse me?"

She stepped out of the embrace, Sirion blushing, "Japheth, this is Seph."

He seemed unconvinced, "He does not even faintly resemble your dog."

Sirion took a deep breath, "If we could step inside, I could explain."

Japheth led them all inside. Once the door was closed, Sirion turned into a dog and back into himself. "I didn't feel it was appropriate for me to be lying at the foot of your bed as newlyweds. So, I left and have come back to help you in this form."

Anekah tried to explain, "He is an angel, dear, and was my protector since birth. He chose the dog form to remain with me incognito. Now he will be with us in this form."

Sirion continued, "That is, if you will allow me to assist you. I am good with machines and with animals. I can help you in the mill to produce the planks needed for the ark. By the way, this is a beautiful gopherwood home."

It was a lot to take in all at once. "We don't have anywhere for you to stay."

He smiled, "That is no problem, I will stay with Regem. Will you allow me to serve you?"

Japheth looked at Anekah, who beamed and nodded hopefully, "Yes of course. We will need all the help we can get."

Chapter Twenty-Seven
At the Mill

The three of them entered the mill. It was a wonder to behold. Outside there had been a stack of gopherwood trees that had been harvested and were ready to be processed, but inside there were two sets of circular saws that Tubal-Cain had manufactured. They were powered by a series of gears. A large spoked wheel lying flat and turned by two horses attached to the gears.

The first order of business every morning, after prayer, was to spray olive oil on all the gears. They ran much smoother that way. Sirion asked Japheth how he knew to spray oil on the gears.

He responded, "That's just what Tubal-Cain said to do and he designed them. I figured that he ought to know."

Sirion just shrugged his shoulders and sprayed away. Then Sirion asked about the two conveyers that delivered the logs to the saws.

"Nope, they operate differently."

"What about the crane that lifts the logs off the pile and onto the conveyer?"

"Ah, they get a light spray of the oil, good catch on that one."

So they sprayed them lightly.

Sirion then questioned, "What do you do with the planks when they come off the second saw?"

"Well," Japheth responded, "We will put them on wagons to deliver to the site where we will build the ark. So far, we have only produced the planks that we used to build our house. We just picked those up by hand and stacked them on the wagons."

"And how long were the planks?" Sirion asked.

"*Hmm,*" Japheth thought a minute. "The studs for the house were on six cubit centers, so the planks would have each been six cubits long."

"But the planks for the ark will be considerably longer than that won't they?" He reasoned, "How will you move them to the wagons?"

Japheth just stood there, "I don't know. We hadn't got that far in the process."

Regem interjected, "Didn't Tubal-Cain make the cranes?" Japheth nodded. "Couldn't he make another one to move the boards to the wagons?"

Japheth looked at the ground, "They are pretty complicated and I think they were difficult to manufacture. He has already helped us so much. I am hesitant to ask him for more help."

Regem blurted out, "Do you have a better idea?"

Japheth still looked at the ground, "I do not. I will ask my father for his opinion after supper Friday night."

They left it at that.

After supper, Japheth sat with his father and Laban in the study.

Noah began, "The preparations for building the ark are going well. We produced a test set of lumber that we used to build Japeth and Anekah's home and that turned out well. However, we have realized that we are not quite prepared to begin production of the planks that will be long enough for the ark. We still need a way to move them from the final saw and onto the wagons that will transport them to the ark's building site. Do you think it would be appropriate to ask Tubal-Cain to build us another crane for that purpose?"

Lahab sat back in his chair and smiled, "It's funny that you should ask. I was talking to Tubal-Cain earlier this week and he was recently visited by a man he befriended from the east. The man had no way to repay him for his kindness at the time Tubal-Cain helped him, but this last week he showed up with two Habbim as gifts for him. He showed them to me. They are large grey behemoths with long trunks for noses. It is reputed that in the east they train them to carry fallen trees with their trunks. I wonder if they could be trained to help you?"

Later that night Japheth was relaying the story to Anekah when she spoke up excitedly, "Habbim? I have never seen one. Are we going to see Tubal-Cain tomorrow?"

Japheth raised his eyebrows, and cocked his head to the left, "I guess we are."

The next afternoon, Tubal-Cain took them out to his stock pens. There stood the two majestic Habbim. Anekah greeted them and the male raised his trunk and trumpeted. They all jumped, except Anekah, who laughed heartedly.

She walked up to the fence and the male, the larger one walked right up to the fence, wrapped his trunk around her under her arms and lifted her from the ground. Startled, Tubal-Cain went to step to her defense, only to meet both Japheth and Sirion's restraining arms. The Habbim lifted his big trunk and deposited her on his neck between his head and shoulders.

Anekah sat back on his shoulders like she had done this all her life and said something they did not recognize. The elephant walked over to a stack of boards on the other side of the fence that were used to replace broken or damaged portions of the fence. He reached over the fence with his trunk, picked up a board and brought it back to the group waiting on the other side of the pen.

Anekah laughed, "Yup, pretty sure that this is going to work." She moved up to the crown of the elephant's head and slid down his trunk to the ground, "Sirion, come here and get acquainted with his wife."

He stepped immediately forward. He had complete trust in Anekah's giftedness.

"Let him smell your hand."

Sirion reached it out and the huge beast reached out his trunk to smell Sirion's hand. His smaller wife had come up along side of him. "Now reach out your hand to her." He did this too and she smelled his hand.

"Now, let him pick you up and place you on his wife."

This was the true test. He just stood there as the huge behemoth wrapped him in his trunk, picked him up, and placed him on the neck of his wife. As an angel, Sirion could communicate with the animals too, but it is always nice to be introduced, first. He asked her to go pick up a fence board like her husband had and she did just that. She lay it down at Anekah's feet. Rather than slide down her trunk, Sirion just raised his leg over her head and slid down next to the elephant's leg.

Chapter Twenty-Eight
Building the Ark

The entire extended family participated in the process of turning the trees into lumber that could be used in building the ark. Tubal-Cain had designed and fabricated the two-man saws used to fell the trees, also the one-man saws his family used to de-limb the trees and prepare them for the milling process. The trees were twenty-five to thirty cubits tall when felled. The tops of them were cut off to leave a twenty cubit log remaining, once de-limbed. These were then stacked in piles. Tubal-Cain's family handled that entire part of the process.

Anekah and Sirion had arrived early that morning to collect the elephants. She addressed Tubal-Cain, "I have a question, what do the Habbim eat?"

Tubal-Cain replied, "A good question. As you know, all the animals eat herbs and vegetables. The Habbim especially like grasses and tree bark, and guess what? They especially love your gopherwood bark. So, where we are felling the trees, and next to the mill, I have placed a bin of grasses and a bin of gopherwood bark that we have ground up to make it more palatable and easy to eat. I have also placed a large container of water for them at those two locations. There should be enough for the entire day and we will refill them each evening after supper."

She took his hands in hers and kissed them. "We will never be able to thank you enough."

The large male Habbim picked her up and placed her on his back, then picked up Sirion and placed him on his wife's back.

Anekah rode the large male Habbim, Mayook, to the tree felling grounds. There, they picked up the logs and placed them on the wagon until the wagon was full. During most of this time, Anekah played a lilting little tune on her flute as she rode joyfully atop the elephant. Her tunes created an atmosphere that made all of their labor much more enjoyable. The wagon then traveled to the mill and was replaced by another that was returning from the mill, and the process continued until they broke for lunch. She led Mayook over to the bins and left him there while she had her own lunch with the other workers.

Sirion rode Akar to the mill and they stationed themselves at the platform that received the finished planks after their final cross-cut. They stood between the platform and the waiting wagon on which they placed the finished planks, pushing them to the far side until the wagon was full. When the wagon was full, it would travel to the area where they were building the ark, to be replaced by another returning.

Taphilla came early one morning with her daughters Mashal and Meshkel, and entertained them with song as they worked. Many of the older ones already knew most of the words. They had been taught by those who sat at the feet of Adam as he recounted them, but they still needed to learn the tune:

> In the beginning was God, and He created
> the heavens and earth.
> The earth was formless and empty, with darkness
> covering its face,
> But the Spirit of God was also there, hovering
> like a mother over the darkness.
> And God said, "Let there be light, and there
> was light, and it was good. That was the first day.

> Then He created the waters, the waters below
> and the waters above,
> Separating the waters below and above,
> making between them a great expanse.
> He called the expansiveness heaven,
> and that became its name.
> That was the second day.

> The third day began with Him moving the waters.
> He moved it until the dry land did appear.
> He called the land, earth, and the waters
> called He seas.
> And all of the earth gave birth to the plants,
> the trees and the plants and all kind of vegetation.
> All that He saw, it too was good.

> The next day He added the stars to the heavens,
> stars for the seasons, for days and for years.
> A bright light for day, a lesser for night,
> all these He placed to rule in the heavens.
> Again, He saw it was good.

The next day the sea brought forth living creatures,
    and birds in abundance filling the air.
He told them to multiply and fill his earth fully.
The sea and the air did their best to comply.
This was another good day.

On this the last day, God called to the earth.
"Bring forth your creatures, cattle and beasts,
    and everything creeping that lives on the ground.
And the earth did respond with each in their kind.
And that too was good.

Finally, God made man in his image.
to rule over all created things.
Male and female He made them all
and blessed them, and commanded them.
Fill earth and lead the earth,
and all that He had made,
all that was filled with the breath of His life.
He looked and looked and looked again
and found that it was all very good.

He rested on the seventh day from all He had done,
from all of the work He had spoken,
and all the things He made.
That day was holy just because, He rested on that day,
He rested, rested, rested, from all of the good
    that He had done.

The song gave them strength and encouragement in their work, for the labor was hard and would prove to be long. Each day Taphilla taught them another song from the teachings of Adam and so, the work became a labor of love. That evening they all went back to their homes and taught the songs to those who had not been at their part of the ark building process. They had repeated it so many times that day and there were enough of them present in each home that they all had it word perfect before the evening ended.

The next day, Taphilla and her daughters taught them a new part of Adam's oral history that they had put to music. Sometimes, after finishing the song for that day there would be questions from different family members. It made the work much less like labor and more like something wonderful, as they all learned more fully the history that only a few of them had completely experienced in person.

Friday evening at family dinner, various family members would share their progress for the week.

After praying, Lahab asked, "So, how does it seem to be going?"

Noah began, "It seems awfully slow, but when the lives of my family and all of the animals are on the line, we want to make sure that we get everything exactly right."

Lamech jumped in, "Which brings up an interesting question. What happens to the rest of us?"

Noah looked down at the table, "I was wondering when that question would be asked again. As I mentioned before we started, when Methuselah dies 'It' will come. The 'it' is most likely the flood. If he will die naturally or be translated like his father was, I do not know. I have asked Rayeh about the rest of you, but so far He hasn't responded. So, I'm not sure."

Sirion raised his hand and Lahab recognized him, "You don't have to raise your hand, Sirion. You are part of us now. Your voice needs to be heard."

Sirion spoke slowly, "While I know that we are mostly self-supporting, yet earlier this week I went into the city for a few specialty items that Tubal-Cain required."

Someone piped up, "He's always needing something special," and there was brief laughter, just enough to cut the tension.

Sirion continued, "Well, the rumors of our building project are running rampant in the city. In fact, I heard that even Prince Lucifer is concerned. He sees us as some kind of threat and is wondering if the project is something with military potential. We should be expecting some investigation, if not some direct opposition."

Chapter Twenty-Nine
Opposition

Anekah and Sirion with the help of the Habbim continued to work with Japheth and the rest of the family on
providing the materials for the ark. The rumors of Lucifer's
concern with their project did turn into confrontations. Lucifer sent Haniel to discover the intent of the project. After his
meeting with Regem and Noah, Haniel assured Lucifer that
what Noah was building was not meant for military purpos-
es, but Lucifer was not convinced. Rather, Lucifer chose to
send Raziel against Noah.

Haniel sent his commander Zadok to warn Noah and was
rewarded with the gift of a Zedekeem, one of the stones of
Rightness. It put Haniel and Regem in direct communication
regardless of the distance, but was only to be used in emer-
gencies.

Raziel attempted to confront Noah, but that proved unsuc-
cessful. In fact, Regem and Noah made him look like a fool.
Raziel's report back to Lucifer was not a pretty sight. Raziel
felt lucky to retain his head when he left that meeting. Lucifer
then tried to gain access to Noah's lands through the suppos-

edly "haunted forest" that surrounded them, but that proved painfully slow. Rayeh's obvious protection kept Noah and his extended family from worrying. All of this did, however, add to the urgency of their task in building the ark.

Lucifer thought, *"Surely if I attack Noah myself..."* but when he did he too was made to look like a fool. Noah told Lucifer of the coming flood and the ark that he was building, but Lucifer, still seated on his horse, laughed maniacally and tried to pull his dark sword. The sword fell from his hand to the ground.

Noah dismounted from his own horse and walked over to the fallen sword.

Lucifer screamed, "Do not touch it!"

Noah picked it up and Lucifer shuddered. It was a thing of beauty, like the seven singing swords forged for the archangels before time began, even in its darkened state. Noah handed it back to Lucifer, but not pommel first. Lucifer had to take it back by the blade and in so doing cut his hand.

In agony, Lucifer cried out, "You fool!" and tried to pull his horse away.

"No," Noah whispered, "you are the fool. You were once the prince of the archangels, but chose to revolt against heaven. You do not rule where I stand and I have not given you leave to go." Noah turned his back on Lucifer, "Now, leave my land!" Noah mounted his horse, joined the other rider, and the two of them began to walk towards Noah's home.

Lucifer just stood there. Finally he whispered to himself, "Who is that who rides with Noah?" His horse turned of its own accord and began to leave with Lucifer on his back.

Raziel spoke hesitantly, "Back to the palace," and they all turned to straggle behind Lucifer and Raziel.

Later, in utter frustration, Lucifer sought to destroy all Noah's relatives, living in the surrounding area. He commanded

Raziel and the five kings to attack them after their preparation for "the day of rest". They usually all came in from the fields to meet together prior to attending the dinner that preceded that day.

A small bird sat perched on the window sill of Anekah's room when she awoke. "Mistress, the armies of Raziel, those not still employed in the forest, and those of the five kings, are set to march against all of Noah's relatives tomorrow." Anekah rubbed her eyes, "Thank you my friend. I will warn Lahab and surely he will send messengers to warn them of the pending attack." The bird flew off and Anekah quickly completed her toilet, dressed, left her home, and went to Lahab's study. Although hesitant to interrupt his morning devotions, she felt this information far too important to wait, "Master, please excuse my impertinence, but may I have a moment of your time?"

Lahab lifted his eyes from the scroll he had been contemplating, "Yes, of course."

She proceeded, her head bowed, "It has come to my attention that there will be an attack against all of Noah's relatives tomorrow."

He folded his hands and rested his chin on them, "That is a good plan on Lucifer's part, since we will be preparing for our day of rest." He looked out the window, "Have Mattan attend me, please." He looked back down to his scroll, "and thank you."

Anekah went to the men's quarters, asked for Mattan, and told him that Lahab had requested his presence. She saw him a few moments later walk purposefully from the study. She heard a few horses gallop away and went back to tell Japheth what was happening.

Chapter Thirty
On the Other Side of Grief

A nekah had been called to Lahab's study. Methuselah sat there looking travel-worn and old, decidedly old. Lahab motioned and she took a seat. Methuselah had been speaking when she entered. He continued, "Thank you for the warning. At least we were prepared. I'm sure they were surprised, maybe even amazed that we did not defend ourselves, but let them slaughter us. I doubt if they had ever faced men, women, and children who were not afraid to die." He smiled weakly, "Because we don't die. We just crossover to that better place, with Him." He pointed up. "Many of the servants had a chance to escape into the forest and then into the hills, but instead chose to be slaughtered with the rest of us. That is because they too would not really die, but simply crossover to be with Him."

Lahab looked dejectedly at the table, "And only you survived?"

He looked up when Methuselah countered, "And you. I'm surprised that you too have not been attacked. You know that you do not enter the ark?"

Lahab sighed, "Yes, I know, but it seems the time of our departure has not yet come. For the time being, the favor covering Noah extends to us also. What about the mourning of our loss?"

Methuselah took a slow deep breath, "There is nothing to mourn. After the slaughter, they put everything to the torch; the people, the livestock, the houses, everything. You are lucky the wind was not blowing in this direction or you would have smelled the stench of this abomination. What have we done to deserve this?"

It was Lahab's turn to take a long sigh, "It was probably an act of mercy that they were all slaughtered quickly and not beaten, tortured, or just burned alive."

Methuselah looked down, "You're probably right. What now?"

Lahab caught Methuselah's eye, "We continue to build the ark. We only have as long as you are alive." He smiled, "So, please keep on living. We still have a lot left to do." He turned to Anekah, "I have heard of the great help you have been to the plank building process, you and your Habbim. How has that been possible?"

Anekah blushed, "Mayook and I are friends," she stated matter-of-factly.

Lahab furrowed his brow, "And how is it that you are friends with a Habbim?"

She was looking at the table, "You know that I can communicate with most animals." she reminded him.

Lahab turned to Methuselah, "Now you see how Noah will be able to get all the animals onto the ark? We have Anekah."

She blushed again, as she added, "And perhaps the aid of some angels."

Methusaleh looked at Anekah, "Not that we should be surprised, but it seems that Rayeh has everything under control. I do have a question though. How will it be determined which animals will be saved on the ark?"

At that moment a sparrow lit on the sill of the window that looked out of the study into the garden. It sang for a moment.

Anekah had looked to the bird as it sang, "It's interesting that you should ask. It seems a council of the animals has been called to discuss that very question. If you will excuse me, I have been asked to attend."

Lahab looked at Methuselah and then back to Anekah, "By all means, and greet them for Methuselah and I." She nodded, rose from her seat, and left.

Chapter Thirty-One
Council of the Animals

When she exited Labah's home, Anekah found Sirion mounted on his stallion, next to her own horse. He held the reigns out to her, "Council of the animals?"

Anekah looked up to him, smiling, "So Soos says. Where are we meeting them?"

"In the haunted forest," and he smiled at the word "haunted."

They found an animal path that you could only find if you had been shown. They followed it until they reached a large clearing. In the center of the clearing was a large circle of thirty stone monoliths, two stones which were in the shape of chairs. The monoliths stood about four cubits wide and six cubits tall.

As they walked towards the gap that contained the chairs, they realized that in the very center of the circle stood a stone table with Rayeh sitting on it. He motioned to Anekah and Sirion to sit in the two stone chairs. As they did, they saw that on the inside of the monoliths were thirty pairs of animals. Anekah and Sirion sat down.

"I have brought you all here to put your hearts at rest." Rayeh seemed more regal than normal. "You know that the end of all flesh is coming before me, but that I will save a remnant on the ark. You are wondering how that final remnant will be chosen. It is simple. You, the current remnant, will remain here in my 'haunted,'" he smiled at the word, "forest and your children's children will bear that last generation that will enter the ark. They will meet here and Anekah and my shepherds will lead them to the ark via that path," and he pointed to a larger path which lay behind the two chairs. Any questions?"

The lion Kilyah spoke what was also on the heart of many, "How will the rest of us die? Will we drown in the flood?"

Rayeh sighed "You will not. After your last generation has entered the ark, that final night you will all fall asleep and when you waken you will be with me," He looked up, "on the other side. Anything else?"

Kilyah ventured one more question, "And Lucifer and his armies?"

A look of sadness crossed Rayeh's face and he looked down to his hands folded in his lap. "All except the Fallen themselves will perish in the flood. Until then he will do his best to penetrate this forest and have a final confrontation at the foot of the ark. You will continue to obstruct his progress, and thank you for your help." With that, Rayeh stood, raised his hands, and blessed them, "Know that I love you all, very much." His pronouncement was met with a cacophony of animal praise in response. A portal opened and he stepped through it.

Chapter Thirty-Two
Finishing

Completing the milling of all the lumber that they thought they would need was a milestone that was finished before the unfortunate massacre of Methuselah's family, servants, and all that they had. That still left many years of assembling the ark. Anekah, Sirion, and their two Habbim were reassigned to hold planks in place while they were attached to the ark. Shem and Meshkel were in charge of the pitch process. They withdrew sap from the gopherwood trees, combined it with charcoal from the fire pits that burned the scraps from the milling process, and cooked it into a texture they could apply to the seams between the planks as they were assembled and then the plank was painted inside and out after it was installed. Once the lower hull was complete they installed the first deck while the rest of the pitch painting was completed. Then it was the next layer of the hull, the next deck, the final layer, the final deck, and the roof.

It seemed like their whole lives consisted of planks and pitch, and then more of the same. If it hadn't been for the songs that they sung to each other they would have gone mad. They did squeeze in a little planting and harvesting though, which was good, because now it was time to gather up the stores of food that would keep them alive on the ark. Finally, the ark stood finished and was filled with stores of food.

Noah addressed them at their evening meal, "I think we are ready to begin filling the ark tomorrow." He faced Anekah, "Will the animals be ready to begin boarding the ark then?"

They all looked a little haggard as they turned to face her, but she perked right up.

"I will have the nocturnals begin gathering tonight, so that we will be ready to board in the morning.

The next morning, Meshkel and Mashal started the song they had composed for the animal procession and out of the forest marched a line of small common animals in pairs: mice, moles, rats, and weasels. They were followed by rabbits, raccoons, cats and dogs. Pairs of birds also accompanied them: ravens, owls, hawks, pelicans, and eagles. This continued until it was time for the intermediate-sized animals and the ramp was repositioned to the second level. Now came the jaguars, lions, horses, even two apes and two monkeys. Then they were followed seven pairs of the following animals, because they were special and not common. They were sheep, goats, deer, antelope and of the birds: doves, pigeons, turkeys, ducks, and geese. This continued until the intermediate deck was filled and they moved the ramp to the lower deck. Then came the pairs of large common animals: two camels, two hippos, two rhinos, two elephants. They were followed by the large special animals; seven pairs of buffalo, ox, cow, until all the animals were aboard. Rayeh had assigned some angels to help shepherd them along the path to the ark and then onto the ark itself. There were no problems other than those usually faced when dealing with youth. What they were gaining in the animals' small size they lost somewhat in discipline, hence the angelic shepherds.

All things considered, it went quite well, probably because there was an angelic shepherd every stadia keeping the animals in line and from acting up too much. Also, it was easier with the larger animals. Even so, at one point the two cats started chasing the two mice and those around them started taking sides. It was quickly turning into general chaos until one of the shepherds went all eight cubits tall and pulled his sword. He walked a couple of them back in line and things settled right down. They had barely gotten in the ark, followed by Noah and his family, including Anekah, when a small portal opened that was filled with Haniel's face.

"Regem," he called.

"I am here," Regem answered.

"Lucifer and his forces have broken through the forest and will shortly attack you." Haniel warned.

"We are prepared. Everyone is already in the ark," but he was wrong.

Anekah had come back out and stood beside him, "Father?"

"Anekah, you are there?" Said an astonished Haniel.

"Yes," she confided, "I have married one of Noah's sons and I will be fine. I love you father."

He began, "and I..." but was cut off as she turned and ran up the ramp into the ark.

Regem explained, "They are here. Goodbye, my friend."

"Rayeh's favor go with you," and the portal closed.

Chapter Thirty-Three
Last Conflict

Lucifer's forces assembled before the ark. There were rows of mounted archers with mounted solders carrying torchers interspersed between them.

Noah had walked back out of the ark when Anekah ran in. He walked up beside Regem on the ramp to face the horde.

Lucifer's two armies assembled before the ark. Lucifer had his stallion step forward and sounded like he was cursing, "Bring everyone back out of that abomination or I will destroy it!"

Noah took one step down the ramp towards Lucifer. "This is not your domain; I forbid you to speak!"

Lucifer tried to speak again, but found that he could not. He began to turn purple with anger, waving his arms and frantically gesturing.

Noah continued, "The end of all flesh is at hand. Water will fall from the skies for forty days and forty nights. The fountains of the deep will open to spew forth water and all the earth will be covered in a flood. All in whom is the breath of life will perish, except those who accompany me on the ark. This is your last chance to join us, come!"

A soldier broke through the ranks, dropping his sword, "I will come!" An arrow pierced him back to front, clean through, and he fell dead to the ground.

"Who loosed that arrow?" commanded Raziel. His commander, Tudar, raised his empty bow. Raziel laughed in derision, "Any others care to join that soldier?" he sneered.

Noah turned and marched back into the ark. Regem walked down off the ramp, stepped aside, and turned into his eight cubit tall angelic self full of glory.

With Noah gone, Lucifer had found his voice and croaked, "R'gal, I slew you in the rebellion."

Another man stepped to the other side of the ramp in his own eight cubits of glory and together, he and R'gal lifted the ramp, slid it into its slot, and closed the large door.

Lucifer yelled, "Arrows," and the archers pulled back their arrows. "Add fire," and the soldiers lit the arrows.

The man who had assisted R'gal turned into the light of the lit arrows. It was Rayeh.

With his back to the ark, Lucifer raised his hand. He yelled, "Fire!" as he dropped his hand, and turned around to face the ark. Lucifer, seeing Rayeh, grabbed his chest and fell off his horse. The flaming arrows hit the ark and did nothing. The ark did not catch on fire. The arrows just burned themselves up.

Raziel, seeing Lucifer on the ground, shouted, "Again," and raised his hand. When he dropped his hand, more flaming arrows struck the ark, and simply burned themselves out.

A portal opened. Rayeh and R'gal walked through it.

Raziel jumped off his horse, ran to Lucifer, and tried to help him up.

Lucifer batted his hands away and struggled to his feet. He raised his hand, there where he stood. "Again!"

More arrows struck the ark, only to burn themselves out. Something about the pitch rendered the ark non-flammable. Again and again they fired flaming arrows into the ark, but to no effect.

"Wait!" Lucifer held up his hand and the volley of arrows stopped. For a moment there was silence. Then Lucifer slowly lowered his hand and began too laugh. "He locked them in." His laughter grew. "He locked them in and left them." He could barely contain himself as the ripples of maniacal laughter spread through his army. "He left them TO DIE!" His indignities forgotten, he turned to his troops and raised his sword high, "We have won! The earth is ours!" Jubilant now, he mounted his horse, turned and yelled mockingly to the sky, "Where is your water from my sky and from the depths of my earth?" He spat on the ground, turned, and rode away to the cheers of his army.

The entire earth celebrated Lucifer's victory in grand debauchery, without restraint for seven whole days while the ark just sat there, an indestructible monument full of burnt-out arrows.

On the eighth day it rained.

Chapter Thirty-Four
Rain

Much of the week before the rains came was taken up in learning how they were all going to live together on the ark. That was difficult when no one knew how long the "trip" would take. Fortunately, they were all dedicated to helping everyone survive the "trip," as they referred to it. The pens were separated by aisles. Next to the aisle and at one end of each pen was a place for food. At the other end was a place for waste. Each day, food would be delivered from the stores on each deck and the waste removed to a lower deck holding area. They all hoped whoever had estimated both the food storage and waste holding had been pretty accurate. Finally the day came. The humans gathered for prayer and Anekah translated for the animals.

Then the rains began. It was a roar that thundered against the outside of the hull and roof of the ark. The sound of the rain blocked out everything and after a while they almost didn't notice it, other than it was difficult for the humans to speak with one another. Since the animals didn't talk out loud it didn't matter that much to them. The sound disguised the horror that there were people outside, banging on the ark, trying to get in. Then the waters rose to a level where they had to swim to survive. Initially as the waters began to rise, a few tried to scavenge unused planks outside the ark. Some even tried unsuccessfully to build rudimentary rafts, but all to no avail. A few tried to float on planks they had found for their own use, but then it became a fight for who would have a plank to float on and they killed one another over their possession.

It rained for forty days and forty nights. Then the rains stopped and the fountains of the deep closed up. A wind began to howl about the ark. Rayeh was drying up the waters. At the end of one hundred and fifty days the ark came to rest on a mountain top. At the end of forty days, Noah released a raven out of the ark's window. It did not return. No one knew why. Noah released a dove, but it returned. Anekah informed them there had been no place for the dove to set her foot. Seven days later he released her again. This time she returned with an olive branch. The waters had receded and life was beginning to appear. He waited one more week, released her again and she did not return. Anekah assured them that she was building herself a nest in the new world.

It was another eight weeks before Rayeh opened the door and said, "Noah, come out, you and your wife, your sons and their wives. Bring with you every living thing in which is the breath of life which we have rescued: all the birds, animals, and everything that creeps upon the earth. Let them be fruitful, multiply, and cover the face of the earth."

They all stood around as Noah and his sons built an altar of unhewn stones. They made sacrifice to Rayeh. Suddenly, he stood there. He promised that he would never again destroy the earth with a flood.

Rayeh said, "I will place my bow in the clouds and it shall be the sign of the covenant I have established for all time, between me and you and all the creatures of the earth." Suddenly the sky was filled with its first rainbow. Rayeh then epeated his final command, "Be fruitful, multiply, and fill the earth." They all stood in silence for a moment then a portal opened and Rayeh walked through it.

They all dispersed to fulfill His command and live in His promise.

Chapter Thirty-Five
Replaced Affections

It has been eighteen years since the flood. Things have returned to a state of normalcy; planting, harvesting, and expanding, as their part in fulfilling the command to "multiply and increase upon the face of the earth."

Anekah was surprised to find that she was fertile. She had been taught that all the Ashareem were sterile, but maybe that only applied to all the others, who were all male. Anekah conceived and bore seven sons to Japheth; Gomer, Magog, Tiras, Javan, Tubal, Meshech, and Madai. Unfortunately, after her last son and the complications that she experienced in his delivery, she was rendered barren. It didn't seem to matter much while she raised little Madai, but once he was weaned, Japheth expected to have another son and she was unable to fulfill that expectation.

While Japheth said that he still loved her and would continue to provide for her, his eye was attracted to Shem's oldest daughter, Sapphire. While young, she was of child-bearing age, and quite a beauty. Before the days of the ceremony,

Anekah was moved out to her own small house, making room for Japheth's new bride.

Anekah sat on her porch enjoying the cool of the day when a stately hound approached.

He sighed, "My condolences on your being replaced."

Anekah smiled, "Seph, it has been far too long."

His voice was laced with laughter, "We have both been busy these last years. You with raising a family and I with trying to help shepherd the animals in their own version of 'multiply and fill the earth.'"

She too laughed, "Yes, a task much larger than we first anticipated."

He walked up and brushed against her leg. She reached down to fondly scratch him.

Seph asked, "What will you do now that you have been relegated to this?" He looked around at the house and its small yard.

She took his chin and looked deeply into his eyes, "Am I sensing an adventure?"

He responded, "We could return to the open road, unless you are too old for that sort of thing?"

She playfully bopped him on the top of the head as she mused, "*The road,*" then out loud, "Has He said anything about what's next?" She looked up.

"Not to me, it's just a feeling. Call it a restlessness, a time to move on."

She stood abruptly, "Come on in while I grab a few things." She went to her bedroom, grabbed a rucksack and began to stuff a few things into it. "Are we traveling light?" she called back to him.

"Probably a good plan," he returned.

"Have you had supper?" she asked as she emerged from the bedroom with a bag over her shoulder.

"Not to speak of."

"Then let me also grab some things we can consume on the way," and she added some fruit and dried meat into another sack.

He added, "You know that as an angel I don't really need to eat."

"Yes," she laughed lightly again, "but you can keep me company." She placed the sack in her bag, laced it up, knelt next to Seph, and laid her hand on his head as she said, "Rayeh, lead us, as we begin this next adventure."

They were a few stadia away from the house when she asked, "Should I have left a note?"

"What would you have said? This will just add to the mystery, 'She came out of nowhere and it seems that she has returned to nowhere.' That is what the story will become."

"Should we sing?"

"Sure why not, just not too loudly."

She took a deep breath and began:

For now the road is level and straight
    as we are walking side by side
This sunshine sure is feeling great
    with only the wind to be our guide
What more is there to ask for
    what more is there that He could give
A pleasant wind is good for sure
    and this is the only way to live.

This ends
the Third Book
of
The Adventures of R'gal
the Archangel

Glossary of Names

Abigail - maid to Judith
Abiel - Lahab's brother
Akar - smaller female Habbim (elephant)
Allon - one of Lahab's shepherds
Anekah - the female Ashereem daughter of
     Haniel and Judith
Araphel - the female Ashereem daughter of Lucifer
Ashereem - the offspring of fallen angels and men
Ashima - Lahab's wife
Balek - one of Lahab's shepherds
Beboni - son of the lion Kilyah
Bedad - Lahab's guard
Bella - Ashima's handmaid
Bohan - one of Lahab's shepherds
Chayeem - the Tree of Life (Laughter)
Dumb - Balek's lead ram
Eder - one of Lahab's shepherds
Elah - Haniel and Judith's half angelic son
Enoch - Jared's son and Japhia's husband
Ham - Noah's son
Haniel - an archangel, the comedian with the sword Hane
Hathath - the fallen angel who sires the Ariel
Japhia - Elah's bethrothed who becomes Enoch's wife
Jashon - one of Lahab's shepherds
Japheth - Noah's son
Judith - Princess and Haniel's wife
Juniel - Noah's servant, friend of Regem (R'gal)
Kilyah - son of the lion Ladub
Kaleph - one of Lahab's guards

Labah - one of the other two Ariel
Labee - the first Ariel produced by Hathath
Ladub - lion friend of Anekah
Laesh - one of the other two Ariel
Lahab - Methuselah's son
Lamech - Methuselah's son, Noah's father
Lucifer - Prince of the archangels, leader of the Fallen
Luthur - An Ariel, Hathath's fourth son
Maliel - Lahab's sister
Mashal - daughter of Taphilla, wife to Noah's son Ham
Mayor - large male Habbim (elephant)
Mehujael - Luthur's soldier
Mekaroth - Raziel's half angel son, head of the Ashereem
Melek - Lahab's master woodworker
Meshkel - daughter of Taphilla, wife to Noah's son Shem
Methuselah - Enoch's son named, "When he is gone
        IT will come"
Naamah - Noah's wife, mother to his three sons
Neseph - Shamah in the form of a dog
Noah - Lamech's son by his wife Adah
Rayeh - the boy in the Tree, teacher of the archangels,
        and...
Rayneh - Adah's granddaughter, wife to Japheth
Raziel - an archangel, the mysterious one with the
        sword Oz-Glory
Regem - R'gal as a man helping Noah
R'gal - one of the archangels, slain in the rebellion
        with the sword Yaman
        -My Right Hand, later with Shenah-Change
Robsar - smithy in the wilderness forging swords
        of wonder
Seph - short for Neseph, Shamah as a dog with Anekah
Shem - Noah's son

Soos - the swallow

Stadia - a measurement equal to about 350 cubits, or 517 feet

Taphilla - daughter of Jubal and Ereveem, with a beautiful voice

Tartak - one of Lahab's shepherds

Tubal-Cain - Lamech's son

Zedekeem - the stones of rightness

Zillah - Lamech's wife, grandmother of Naamah, who was Noah's wife

About the Author

William Siems, "Bill" to his friends, seems to have started telling stories as soon as he could talk. His wife says he still tends to share the truth creatively and with a flair for the dramatic. He grew up in south Seattle and has lived in Tacoma, Washington since 1972.

He worked nine years in hospitals, completing half his RN education. If you had a heart attack, he says he could half save you. Bill joined the Boeing Airplane Company in 1979. The last 15 years of his 32-year career he taught Employee and Leadership Development. Bill often developed and taught his own material. This led to writing numerous short stories and dramas, culminating in his first published novel *Amidst the Stones of Fire* in 2017 and its sequel *Out of the Sanctuary* in 2018. A Biblical Adventure series followed, named *The Chayeem Chronicles*. It began with the Christmas adventure *The Magi and a Lady,* and then the gospel adventures *Hane and the Centurion,* and *Zach and a guy named Joe,* a rewriting of the first part of the book of Acts. This is the finale of his archangel trilogy that began with *The Adventures of R'gal the Archangel,* called *The Sword Shenah* and was followed by *The Prince and the Soldier.* He has also authored a contemporary Christian trilogy *Before the End.*

Now retired, Bill spends his time teaching, mentoring, writing, acting in community theater, and enjoying his family. Bill and his wife Nancy, of more than fifty years, live near their three children, eight grandchildren, and finally a great-grand-daughter.

If you can't find Bill in his home office, with pages from his next book strewn all over the floor, then he used to be across the street playing with the neighbor's dog, Stacy, to whom he is Dogfather. She has gone to a better place, yes he believes in doggie heaven. She is the main character of *Lucy a Dog and Her Friends,* Book Three of the contemporary Christian trilogy.